CW01666816

Marion Zimmer

The Brass Dragon

From the moment Barry wakes up in a strange hospital bed, events take an extraordinary and terrifying turn. Suffering from total amnesia – the only clues to his past are a pair of overalls and a brass dragon – he begins to retrace his steps. The story unfolds in gripping intensity as he learns how he was captured by an alien race and abandoned on Mars with his fellow Galactic citizens – hunted by the *dikri*, the shape-changers, whose dragon-like appearance terrifies anyone who sees them. . . .

MARION ZIMMER BRADLEY

The Brass Dragon

A Methuen Paperback

This title also published in hardback

First published in Great Britain 1978
by Methuen Children's Books Ltd
11 New Fetter Lane, London EC4P 4EE
Text copyright © 1969 by Marion Zimmer Bradley
Published by arrangement with Charter Communications Inc
All rights reserved
Jacket artwork copyright © 1978 Methuen Children's
Books Ltd
Printed in Great Britain by
Cox & Wyman Ltd, London, Reading and Fakenham

ISBN 0 416 86370 1

*This paperback is sold subject to the condition that
it shall not, by way of trade or otherwise be lent,
re-sold, hired out, or otherwise circulated without
the publisher's prior consent in any form of binding
or cover other than that in which it is published
and without a similar condition including this condition
being imposed on the subsequent purchaser*

To David
who saw the Brass Dragon in Texas

Part I

CHAPTER ONE

'No, Rellin!'

The scream crashed through the silence, and I woke up.

I sat up, blinking, and pain thundered through my head like the scream. My head felt huge, as if it were something balanced precariously on my shoulders. I eased the clumsy thing back down to the pillow, and cautiously slitted my eyes open again.

People screaming all over the place! Might as well be in the nut house. Instead of – I blinked again and came all the way awake:

This wasn't my bedroom!

The walls were white, and the window was white, too, and not curtained. There were venetian blinds, and thick sunlight made streaks through them and lay, in yellow barred glare, on the wall. The glare hurt my eyes, and I shut them again. Where was I? And why were people screaming all over the place, so loud that it might as well be right in the–

For God's sake, it *was* right in the room!

I had screamed.

I put my hands up to my face. Where was I, and what was going on? I touched my face, and then I had the second shock:

My face was rough. I had a beard.

A *beard*? At my age? I'd shaved about twice in my life. That wasn't bad, for seventeen, but here I was with my chin rough and scratchy with a full-grown beard. *Where was I? What had happened?*

The door opened, and a nurse came into the room, and things suddenly clicked and fell into place.

Accident. I had had an accident, and I was in a hospital. Maybe a car had hit me on my way home from school–

The nurse was dressed in white, like most nurses. She was dark, and pretty, and smiling. 'Is something wrong?' she asked.

Wrong? Was anything *right*?

'I heard you cry out again – that *was* you, wasn't it?'

'Oh. Oh, yes, that was me.'

'Have you been dreaming again?' She sounded concerned.

Again? What was that supposed to mean? 'I'm sorry. I'm feeling pretty dim just now. Have I been screaming before this?'

She nodded. 'Yes. Don't you remember? Last night you woke up three times, shouting something about a railing. Can you remember now what it was? Did you fall through a railing, perhaps?'

'I don't know,' I said slowly. 'I assume I'm in a hospital. Is this Herrick?'

She nodded, smiling. 'Yes, this is Hendrick Hospital. So you know where you are? That's wonderful. Perhaps you'll remember, in a little while, what happened, and what all this is about railings.'

I frowned, and wished I hadn't: it hurt. It didn't sound like me. I didn't have nightmares, and I hadn't screamed since I was thirteen and slammed my fingernail in the car door. Why could I remember that, and not anything closer? Railings? I racked my brain, trying to remember what it was that I'd screamed – or dreamed. I couldn't remember, but for some strange reason I was sure it had nothing to do with a railing.

'Dr Bannon said he wanted to see you when you woke up,' the nurse said. 'I'll call him,' she added as she went out.

Dr Bannon? I'd never heard the name. I rubbed my hand against that strange wrongness of my face again, mostly because it kept me from thinking. Somewhere at the back of my mind I was beginning to get scared.

There was something wrong. Something I halfway knew about, and didn't dare think about yet. I knew that if I let myself think about it, that vague little bit of fear at the back of my mind would come roaring out like a tiger and I'd start screaming the place down again.

After a while, the door swung quietly open again, and a man stood in the door.

I'd never seen the man before, but I knew by his white coat that he was a doctor. He was youngish, with grey eyes and dark hair, and he frowned a little as he looked at me. Was I hurt as badly as all that?

'Miss Taylor tells me you've decided to wake up,' he said pleasantly, but his eyes stayed fixed right on me. 'How do you feel now?'

Experimentally, I moved. No casts, nothing seriously damaged or out of place, though there was something stiff and rustly on the calf of my leg that felt like a bandage, and my elbow felt queer. 'My head aches a bit. Apart from that, I guess I'm okay. What happened, anyway? An accident?'

'We were hoping you could tell us that,' he said

slowly. 'We don't know; a policeman found you lying in the street and brought you to the emergency room. We took X-rays to make sure your skull wasn't fractured; otherwise you're not badly hurt except for something like a burn on your leg and one temple. Frankly, I can't quite imagine what sort of accident – but no, you're not badly hurt. You should be all right in a day or two.'

'That's good,' I said, but unease was building up inside me again. I wasn't hurt badly, maybe, but there was *something–*

'But now that you're awake and can talk sensibly, maybe you can tell us,' Dr Bannon said. 'What happened?'

I tried thinking back, but it was like trying to remember what I'd screamed. There was a curious, fuzzy sense of fear, and a great crash that seemed to fill the sky . . .

'There was a crash,' I said slowly, 'and – and something must have hit me – but I can't remember. I can't remember!'

'Easy, easy,' the doctor said hastily. 'Don't get excited. It will come back to you. With a head injury, sometimes there's a memory lapse. Suppose we get the rest straight first. There was no identification on you, you know, so we haven't even been able to notify your family. First of all – who are you?'

And then it crashed in on me, and I knew what it was that I hadn't wanted to feel. Why I'd kept my mind busy with so many unimportant questions. And why I'd held so many questions back.

Who are you?

A simple enough question. The first thing they always ask.

There was nothing wrong with the question, just with the answer.

I didn't know who I was.

I didn't know my own name!

I guess my face must have done something I didn't know about. Because the next thing I knew the nurse was there with a little paper cup of something that smelled funny, and Dr Bannon was saying 'Hey, hey, take it easy, kid!'

I just lay there, feeling stunned and sick. The nurse held the paper cup insistently to my mouth and I swallowed without arguing. Arguing wouldn't do any good, anyhow.

'That, that – I mean – I've got to *know*,' I stammered. 'It doesn't make sense–'

'Don't worry about it,' Bannon repeated. 'Above all, don't get excited. It happens sometimes with a head injury. I'm sure you'll remember–'

A word flickered in my mind. 'Amnesia,' I said, interrupting the doctor's flow of words. 'Have I got amnesia? But I thought people forgot everything, so if I've forgotten my own name how do I know what amnesia is?'

He smiled. It made him look human, and likeable. 'Oh, there are different forms of amnesia,' he said. 'So you've heard the word, though? That's interesting. And you know what it means. Well, maybe you should know enough not to worry, then. Sometimes people forget just the things connected with their accident. Sometimes–'

But I didn't listen, because I knew what he was doing. He was just talking to keep me from panicking, from yelling and screaming like a little kid.

What was the matter? Who was I?

I said helplessly, 'Why can't I remember my *name*?' and heard my voice crack.

'What *can* you remember?' The doctor sounded calm and soothing. 'Miss Taylor said you knew where you were.'

'I'm in a hospital. Is it Herrick Hospital?'

Now he looked at me, startled. 'No,' he said, 'it's *Hendrick* hospital. Do you know where that is?'

'Hendrick? I never heard of it,' I said, confused. 'Herrick is in Berkeley.' I added, after a minute, 'Berkeley, California. Is this hospital in San Francisco?'

Dr Bannon nodded. 'Now we're getting somewhere,' he said. 'Do you live in California? Or – isn't Berkeley where the university is? Are you a student there?'

'No,' I said, 'I'm not in college. Please, where is this?'

'Take it easy,' Dr Bannon said. 'Hendrick Hospital is in Abilene, Texas.'

Abilene, Texas! I lay back, feeling a little sick. I'd never been in Texas in my life.

'I must have lost some time,' I said. 'What day is it?'

'What day do you think it ought to be?'

'June 4th, 1967–' I shook my head, forgetting the bandage, and winced again. 'Did I miss my – what day is it?'

Dr Bannon went out into the hall. He returned immediately with a newspaper in his hand. The *Abilene Daily News*. He pointed, silently, to the date:

September 2, 1968.

A year and three months!

‘And when was I brought in here?’

‘It’s Saturday now. They brought you in Wednesday night.’ He smiled. ‘What’s the last thing you remember?’

Off in a corner of my mind there was something white, like– ‘An albino dwarf,’ I said. ‘No, that doesn’t make sense– Nothing. I’m sorry.’

‘Nothing to be sorry about.’ Bannon was soothing me again, calming me down, and I wished he wouldn’t; I wanted to take this seriously.

‘We’ve done some checking,’ he said. ‘You’re not from the Army or the Air Force, and you weren’t wearing any military dog tag, so I don’t imagine the Navy or the Marines will claim you either; but it was worth checking. Missing Persons in Texas had nothing on any boy near your age. We have two leads. Give me that thing out on the desk,’ he said to the nurse. When she went out to get it, he said, ‘So you’re from California. Have you lived there long? We can check with Missing Persons there, you know.’

The nurse came back with a long yellow sheet.

‘It’s routine, when we get anyone unidentified, to check with military AWOL lists, and Missing Persons,’ he said. ‘The police teletypes send out bulletins. Now, there are dozens of juveniles reported missing every month, but we could eliminate quite a number of them right away. And remember anything later than ’67– Let me see – Portland, Maine, white male, blond, sixteen years old. Nels Angstrom– I think we can rule him out. You’re not blond.’

I frowned. ‘I don’t *think*– Nels Angstrom didn’t sound right.’

‘From Los Angeles, wanted for armed robbery,

Pedro Menendez – no, you're not Mexican, and I doubt if you're as much as twenty. From Seattle, Lloyd Sanderson, age eighteen, white, male, American, brown hair, dark eyes – that might be you; reported missing two months ago. We've wired the juvenile authorities in Seattle. Let me see – Berkeley, California, Barry Francis Cowan, age seventeen, missing from May '67, five-foot-eight – well, you could have grown an inch. We wired Mr Cowan, and he said he would fly in tonight just on the chance, but he said he'd made four flights already, to New York, and a couple of other places, to identify someone claiming to be his son. So if you're Cowan or Sanderson–'

'I don't know,' I said, and felt like crying. 'Juvenile authorities?'

'It's routine when someone turns up missing,' the doctor said quickly; 'it doesn't mean you've committed a crime.'

'Did I have anything at all on me when I came in? I mean – no wallet, keys, money?'

'Just the clothes you had on, and a couple of pieces of junk in the pockets,' Dr Bannon said.

'Can I see the clothes?'

'Get his clothes,' Bannon said to the nurse, and she went to a locker at one end of the room. She took out a brown coverall, and laid it across the bed. I eased my head up and took it in my hands.

It was rough and brown, woven of something like denim. Pants and shirt were all in one piece, and it zipped up the front. He said, 'It looks as if something had been ripped off the arm. That's why we checked the Army and Air Force.'

I turned it over in my hands. The rough looking

material felt curiously soft to the touch. Without quite knowing why, I turned it over to the breast pocket, and frowned. Something had been ripped from that, too. It was a large irregular patch of lightish fabric. The nurse said, 'Oh, yes. It could be an eagle or something.'

I shook my head. 'I was wearing *this*?'

'You don't recognize it?'

'Sorry. Where did it come from?'

'I don't know,' Bannon confessed. 'As I say, I thought it might be uniform stuff – that material's amazingly strong and light, so of course I thought of the Armed Forces. But they said no. It might have been made overseas, of course. And of course, with all the new synthetics–' He shrugged.

'What about the pockets?' I demanded impatiently.

He opened a drawer in the night table beside the bed, and took out a small object.

'Eighty cents in silver – it's downstairs in an envelope – and this thing.'

He handed it to me. It was about the size of a rabbit's foot, brass, and it was a little dragon. About two inches long, but a dragon, a brass dragon–

With a sharp intake of breath, I dropped the trinket on the bedclothes and grabbed up the coverall again. Examining the darkish ripped patch, I held it against the brass dragon. Yes. The patch was clearly dragon-shaped. Not an eagle. A dragon. I turned out the inside of the shirt with trembling fingers. There were still threads on the inner side, and the material showed signs of weakening there.

Why had the emblem been ripped off?

I picked up the Brass Dragon – strange, how I

capitalized it in my mind – and examined it, with a feeling of horror. I didn't like touching it.

It was about two inches long. There was a small slot-shaped extrusion at the bottom, and I looked carefully at it, squinting my eyes, for anything that might say *Made in USA* or *Made in Japan* or anything of the usual kind. There was nothing. I rubbed my finger over the slot. Something had been broken from it, too; there was a rough spot there. And the dragon . . .

It seemed to grow, to fill the whole room– Without thinking, I screamed. And screamed again.

'No! *Rellin, no!*'

And everything went a lovely velvet black.

CHAPTER TWO

When I woke up the next time, there were rails around the bed. I examined them for a minute, then lay back and decided I deserved it. If I was going to act like a nut, they'd have to treat me like one. What had got into me, to fly off the handle that way? I felt like a loaded gun with the safety catch off; anything might happen at any time. I didn't like the feeling one bit.

'Awake again?' A very young nurse popped her head in the door. This one had red hair, cut short enough so that only two or three stray curls peeked out under the cap; and instead of a full uniform she had on something like a blue-and-white striped bib apron. The little pin on the front of the apron said *Lisa Barnard*. 'Are you feeling better? I'm sorry, I don't know your name–'

'Neither do I,' I said, grinning for the first time since this had started, and her face turned so red that the freckles looked pink.

'Oh, I'm sorry – I mean–'

'Forget it,' I said. 'I thought I might as well get a couple of laughs; there isn't much else that's funny about this business.' I laughed, and after a minute the little nurse giggled too.

'I *am* sorry. They did tell me you'd had a head injury and hadn't been able to identify yourself yet. Are you able to sit up, Mr–'

'Just call me Mr X, the famous international spy,'

I said, and hauled myself up on my elbow. My head still hurt, but I felt better. Maybe the old guy who said laughter was the best medicine had something after all. I couldn't remember his name, but it didn't bother me. If I couldn't remember my own name, why bother with his?

'I'm Lisa Barnard,' she said, trying to be prim and dignified, but on her it didn't look good, and the perky smile was there behind it.

I put a hand on one of the bed rails and shook it. 'What's with this business – a bed with barred windows?'

She giggled again. 'Oh, that. You were thrashing around in your sleep, and I think they were afraid you'd fall and hurt your head again. So they had me put the rails on the bed.' She popped out into the hall again and came back carrying a tray.

'I knew it was too good to be true,' I said dismally. 'What's on the hospital programme now?'

She chuckled. 'Cheer up. We're going to take off a few of those whiskers, that's all.' She picked up an electric razor.

'You don't approve of beards?' I asked, laughing, and she laughed back.

'I couldn't care less. But Dr Bannon thinks we'd better shave it off so that your father – if it is your father – will be able to recognize you.'

'Aw, shucks,' I said. 'How can I be Ivan X, the mysterious spy, without my beard?'

'It will grow back,' she said primly. It was the funniest thing, the way she'd giggle like one of the girls at my school and all of a sudden she'd have all the dignity you associated with a nurse forty years old. Suddenly I felt depressed. My school. In Berkeley? Yes;

and probably my whole class had gone on and graduated, and all my friends–

'Look,' she said gently, and laid her small hand on my arm. 'You mustn't worry about things. It's going to be all right. A lot of people who get knocks on the head forget things for a while. One morning you'll wake up and remember everything all at once. Honest! I've seen it happen, and I've heard older nurses talking about it.'

'How old are you?' I asked suddenly.

'Eighteen. I've been in training four months–' Suddenly the prim nurse-face slid down like a mask over the girl-face again. 'Come on,' she said with brisk cheerfulness. 'Let's get on with the shave.'

'Sure. Maybe I'll recognize my own face without the beard,' I said a little sourly, and watched her pick up the razor. It buzzed madly when she put it against my face, and she stopped short.

'What am I doing? I'd better trim it off first with scissors.' She took a pair from her pocket and snipped, turning my face this way and that with firm, capable small hands. Then she put up the razor to my face, and this time it behaved properly. She finished the job off with some sort of tart-smelling lotion, and handed me a mirror.

'Feel more like yourself now?'

But it was just a face. I knew it was mine, but that didn't do much good.

'Now,' she said briskly, handing me a blue cotton bathrobe, 'you can get up and walk to the bathroom – it's right in there. Want some help?'

'No, thanks, I can manage,' I said, my face burning and not from the shaving lotion. Maybe she was a nurse, but she was still a young and pretty girl. If it had been the old battle-axe, old enough to be my mother, maybe I wouldn't have felt that way. She saw me blush, and smiled gently, not giggling, as I swayed on my feet.

'Let me know if you want help,' she said kindly, 'And I'll call one of the orderlies or male nurses to give you a hand.'

'Oh.' I felt foolish.

'The doctor says you can have a shower, and then something to eat, and then perhaps you'd like to put some clothes on and sit up,' she said. 'Try walking up and down the corridor a little; that will help you to get your legs under you again.'

I felt a little dizzy when I moved, but I found out that I could walk without help. After a warm shower I felt better; it seemed to take out the kinks in my muscles. I put the cotton robe on again and took a turn up and down the corridor; but by that time I was glad to get into bed and lie back. I was more tired than I thought. I felt as if I'd taken a beating. The windows were closed, and the hospital room was dark. I shut my eyes and tried to think, to remember.

Images, grey and blurry, drifted through my mind. Faces none of which meant anything to me. Slamming my finger in the door of the car when I was thirteen. I'd had to go and have the bone scraped later, and afterwards the doctor had diverted me by showing me an articulated skeleton of a hand, which opened and closed on wires. A ring of faces, sitting around a campfire, singing. The outline of a bridge against the sky; I knew it was the Golden Gate Bridge. Myself walking along a lane between overhanging rhododendron bushes. Myself again, walking across dry desert country, my breathing-mask rough and clammy against my chin, shielding my eyes from the fierce orange glare of the giant overhead. The sharp, rocking impact of take off and then the slow return of sight, and the starburst glare of space beyond the quartz dome . . . a burst of orange fire, searing bright and leaving the retina darkened for minutes . . .

I rocked myself awake, shaking my head, at the farrago of memories. That was no good. If my own memories could get mixed up with some science-fictional TV play, what was the good of trying to free-associate to my own past? Spaceships, for heaven's sake! Next thing, I'd be seeing myself on horseback with Hopalong Cassidy. How was it, I wondered, that I could remember watching television when I was five years old and not remember my own family, or who I'd watched it with? Some of the doctor's words, which I hadn't thought I was listening to at the time, came back to me: lacunary amnesia, usually connected with some head injury, blanked out only selective areas in the memory. For instance, a man he'd known once had fallen out of a third storey window. The man had been a teacher of French; when he came to himself, he could still read French but couldn't speak a word of it.

I heard soft steps in the hall, and Lisa Barnard came quietly into the room. 'Are you asleep? A man who claims to be your father is here. Do you feel up to seeing him?'

I wasn't so sure. Right now I wouldn't have known my father from Adam. The phrase popped into my mind and then I realized I wasn't so sure who Adam was, either. This wasn't good. If there was anybody who could straighten out this mess, I'd sure be glad to see him! It just might be that the minute I laid eyes on him, my whole past would pop back into being. I certainly hoped so.

'Bring him on,' I said.

Lisa turned back to someone in the hall. 'You can come in now, Mr Roland,' she said, and I waited, realizing that my heart was pounding slightly. I heard heavier steps, and then a man came into the room – and my excitement subsided slowly.

I had never seen the man before – at least, not to my knowledge.

And yet – I hesitated. There was some haunting familiarity about him, and strangely, it was not a pleasant familiarity. If this was my father, the thought flashed through my mind, I'm not surprised at myself for running away.

He was tall and heavily built, with swarthy skin and dark eyes, but there was something else about him, something I couldn't identify; the best way I could put it to myself was that he looked as if he were dressed in someone else's clothes. Not that I was any judge of clothes; I just knew that the clothes he was wearing now – a dark business suit, nothing remarkable about it, though the collar opened to accommodate the bulging of enormous neck muscles, and his tie-knot dangled loose a few inches below the collar – didn't suit him. I thought that over a minute, trying to think what *would* suit him, how he *would* look right. In uniform, maybe? A policeman's uniform, a Roman legionary's armour? I couldn't put my finger on it. But I didn't like it – and I didn't like him.

The silence had stretched out long enough to be awkward but Mr Roland still stood, looking down at me, without speaking. I wondered what he was waiting for, and had the distinct feeling that he wanted me to speak first. I decided I wouldn't, I'd just wait for him.

The silence went on stretching out. This was ridiculous. I bit my lip. 'If you're waiting for me to cry out "Daddy" and rush into your arms, it's no good,' I blurted out. 'As far as I know, I've never seen you before in my life.' *And don't care if I never do again.*

'Barry,' he said ruefully, shaking his head. 'I don't think it's necessary to bring the hostility between us out in a place like this.' I had the feeling that he was answering the part of the remark I hadn't made out loud, but the tone was familiar enough. 'I've been worried about you, son. Are you feeling all right now?'

'I'll live,' I said. 'Physically, that is. I guess they told you I don't remember anything.'

Mr Roland turned to the nurse. 'Well, that's that. Of course, he's my son. I assume he can be moved; will you get his clothes, please, and we'll go?'

'Hey,' I protested. 'Not quite so fast!' In the first place I didn't want to be pushed into going with this guy. I didn't recognize him, I felt sick and – yes, damn it, scared. The only familiar things in a bewildered world were this hospital room, Lisa and Dr Bannon, and I wasn't ready to cut adrift from them just yet. 'Right away?'

'Why not?' Roland asked logically. 'What else is necessary and why stay here? Where should you be, except with your father?'

'There are a few formalities,' Lisa said slowly, 'but I don't suppose they'll take very long. Since you do definitely identify him as your son . . .?' She paused, but with the uplift of a question in her voice, and the big man said impatiently, 'Yes, yes, of course.'

'Well, then–' she began, but I broke in. 'But I *haven't* definitely identified *myself* as his son! Do I have to go with him on *his* say-so?'

'Barry, don't be paranoid,' the man admonished sharply, then softened his voice. I had the impression of a film of sticky oil spread over dirty rough rock. He said in a conciliating voice to Lisa, 'I suppose he's afraid of being scolded or punished for running away.' The tone effectively reduced me to a twelve-year-old hiding from a spanking. 'Come, come, Barry, if I were to say that all is forgiven–'

'I don't believe you,' I said roughly. 'I don't think you have the right to forgive me anything, and I'm not going unless you can prove *your* identity to *my* satisfaction. Don't I have any rights here?' I clutched at a faint hope. 'Doesn't the doctor have to sign me out, or anything?'

Lisa looked at me with what seemed like a look of pity. She said, 'It's true that Dr Bannon has to release you formally. Shall I call him?'

'Why is all this necessary?' the man grumbled, and the little nurse said primly, 'Because if he is released, and has a relapse, the hospital is legally responsible. It won't take a minute. Why don't you sit here and have a nice visit with your son, Mr Roland? I'll have Dr Bannon paged.'

She buzzed off, and I lay staring at the window, not looking at the big man who claimed to be my father. I couldn't imagine having a nice visit with that character.

'What's the matter with you, Barry?' the man asked, after a brief silence. 'I thought your memory was gone. How can you possibly have anything against me?'

I countered with another question. 'How did you know I was here?'

'It was broadcast on TV,' he said slowly. 'They appealed for anyone who knew you to come forward.'

The cautiousness of the answer didn't surprise me. I knew he was hiding something and I hadn't expected anything else. I said, 'Tell me about the family.'

'Family?' For a moment I had caught him off guard. I had the feeling that didn't happen often and that he didn't like it; in the fast dark stare he gave me, I realized I'd probably be sorry for it. But his tone was neutral when he spoke. 'I had forgotten you wouldn't remember,' he said. 'Of course your mother is – is dead, and you have no brothers and sisters. Just you and me.'

The words were fine. Only why did they give me the cold chills? I shut my mouth, resolved not to say anything more, and didn't, until Dr Bannon came back.

'Mr Roland, is it? And you've identified your missing son?' he asked. 'Just a few questions. How long has he been missing?'

'Three weeks,' Roland said, with a quick glance at me.

'Why didn't you report him to Missing Persons?'

He had an answer for that one too. 'You know how young people are,' he said, with what was meant to be an understanding smile. 'I thought he would return of his own free will. Now, of course, I know he was not able.'

I said, 'I've been away longer than three weeks,' and looked appealingly at Dr Bannon. Bannon frowned slightly and said, 'If you'll wait outside a minute, sir–'

'Now look here,' the man said, advancing on Bannon with an air of menace. 'This my son, and I have a right to take him home without all these formalities! If you people attempt to prevent me, I shall make trouble!'

I suddenly put my finger on what was wrong. His own speech was too formal, as if he'd learned it from a book. Why did he say 'formalities' instead of 'red tape'? His dialogue wasn't convincing! I started to say so – and, looking up with my mouth open, met his eyes.

I can't explain it. Something in them made me wither like a sensitive plant left out too long in the sun. They were dark eyes, and I had the feeling, looking into them, that I couldn't look away unless he let me . . .

He said, very softly and not bullying at all, 'Clothe yourself, Barry, and we will leave. This person cannot prevent you.'

Dr Bannon said, 'I understand your – son? – still has some objections.'

Roland said suavely, 'Ask him, Barry–?'

I said automatically, 'Yes–?'

'As you will see, he knows his name. Now' – Roland's voice suddenly snapped like a whip – 'request him to become clothed at once and leave here!'

Bannon wasn't going to be bullied. 'Wait outside, then, while he dresses,' he said, and when Roland went into the hall, he turned to me. I sat slumped over in bed, feeling a slow paralysis of despair. Bannon couldn't help me. I'd have to go with him, and then–

'Barry,' Bannon said softly.

'Yes, sir?'

'It *is* your name, obviously,' Bannon pointed out, in a gentle voice. 'What's the matter, son?'

I wished that the 'son' were more than a phrase. It meant more when Bannon said it. I said, in a stifled voice. 'He's not my father,' feeling my throat drying as I spoke. My heart was banging, and the doctor looked at me with concern. 'You're frightened! Yet he knew you, Barry. He knew your name.'

'He *said* he knew me,' I muttered.

'Look,' the doctor urged, 'why should he claim you if he isn't a relative? If you were the heir to a big fortune, or some such thing as that, you would have been claimed before this. There would have been national headlines, if you were the victim of a kidnapping or anything like that. What are you afraid of?'

I didn't know. But I knew when I was licked. Bannon couldn't help me and I couldn't help myself. I sank down on the bed, reaching for the denim coverall, but before I could get it on I started to tremble, and kept on shaking until the thing fell from my hand on to the floor. The greyness started to close in around me again; I saw and felt my hand shaking and I heard Bannon's voice, suddenly high, raised with fear or concern, shouting; but the words slid past me where I huddled in a blind, unthinking terror.

'Barry! Listen to me!' Bannon's hand clamped hard on my arm. 'Take it easy! Listen, kid; I won't release you against your will. If it hits you like that, you're obviously in no shape to leave the hospital anyhow, and I couldn't conscientiously sign you out! Come on, calm down!' His hand eased me back on the pillows as his words slowly filtered through to me. I swallowed, trying to get words out.

Bannon knew what I wanted to say. 'You don't want to face him again? All right, son; I'll tell him that you're not fit to leave the hospital.'

I felt the world settle down again, and slowly my pounding heart quieted to normal. I wet my lips; Bannon poured me a glass of water, handed me a small paper cup with a couple of pills. 'Here, take these. It's just a very mild sedative, but you need it. I'll tell him to come back in a day or two; by then you'll be feeling better. You may even have your memory back.'

I muttered, ashamed, 'Sorry to make – such a scene–'

'Blame *this*,' Bannon said firmly, touching the bandage on my head. 'It's the most natural thing in the world. You lie back and rest, now.'

'Doctor–' I said, as he was going out of the room. 'Tell him – if he comes back – tell *him* to bring some proof! Tell him to bring my – my–' I fumbled for elusive words, thoughts, memories, through the blankness. 'Tell him to bring my – my birth certificate or a picture of me. Or – or some proof that I'm still a minor, or – something like that.'

Bannon raised his dark eyebrows, but said only, 'I'm glad your mind is working as clearly as this; obviously your memory is right under the surface. But don't try too hard. Relax, now, and give that stuff a chance to calm you down.'

He went out, and after a minute, I heard his voice in the corridor, and Roland's, raised, angry, baffled; it went on for some time, and finally subsided and died away down the hall. I began to breathe freely again. Bannon had managed to get rid of him. But for how long?

The sedative he had given me was evidently powerful, no matter what he said. I felt drowsy – or was that just the reaction after my attack of panic? I felt ashamed of it, in a strange way. I ought to have been more coherent, more sensible; I ought to have given good reasons for not wanting to go with that guy – instead of going into hysterics like a silly kid! Dr Bannon must think I was an awful crybaby!

I still felt sheepish when, a little later, Lisa popped in. 'Suppertime,' she said briskly, but I could hardly look at her. Had she heard about me throwing a fit? But she was perfectly natural. 'Dr Bannon told me to check and see if you were awake and hungry; you'd had a sedative, and he said not to wake you up, if you were asleep, but if you were awake, feed you. How hungry are you?'

I thought about that and decided I was pretty hungry. 'I could eat a horse.'

Lisa giggled. 'I don't know if the kitchen has any horses in stock,' she said. 'Would you settle for a plain old chunk of cow or sheep?'

'Just cut off the horns and hooves,' I said gravely, and her mock-solemn smile came again.

'Why, is there something wrong with your teeth? You don't want a nice chunk of horn and hoof pie? Okay, I'll do the best I can.'

When supper came, it wasn't Lisa who brought it, but a pleasant old grey-haired motherly type, and it was some kind of stew, with other things like a salad and toasted muffins and some pudding quite inoffensive and all completely blah. Just the same, I was hungry enough to eat up everything on the tray, and when I shoved it aside, as an exercise in memory, I tried to make myself remember what I would rather eat. Steak. I remembered steak. Maybe a nice cold shrimp cocktail. Hot biscuits. Chili. Chocolate cake or maybe lemon pie.

I branched out a little then. Berkeley, California. I remembered Berkeley. I remembered hikes in the hills, up towards Strawberry Canyon, and the Botanical Gardens back there. But hikes with whom? I must have had a family, teachers, sisters and brothers, yet my mind seemed to be swept clean of *people.*

Go back to the beginning. Had I a house? Blast it, there was nothing but a blank spot. I knew what a house was, but I couldn't remember having one. Clothes, then. Could I remember any clothes? Yes, I remembered wearing a cowboy suit when I was about five. Great, I told myself cynically; just great, I could remember something when I was five. My head ached as if it would burst, and I had, again, that sense of something vast and frightening just past the curtain of memory. Clothes. The brown denim coverall I had been wearing, the little brass dragon– Abruptly I discovered I was sitting bolt upright in bed, my heart pounding. What was it about that thing that scared me, and how did I happen to have something in my pocket that would scare the wits out of me like that?

I knew the doctor wouldn't approve of this. He'd told me not to work too hard at trying to remember; either my memory would come back without me doing anything about it at all, or it wouldn't. But he ought to try it, I thought resentfully, not being able to remember his own name, and see how calm and casually he could take it!

Barry. *Was* my name Barry? Why not – I groped for other names – why not James, or Karsten, or Michael, or Varzil, or John or Richard? Did any of them sound right? Or familiar? Yes, they all sounded equally familiar – and equally unfamiliar.

Oh, nuts. This wasn't getting me anywhere.

Fortunately, before I wound myself up too far into knots, Dr Bannon came in again. He looked at me with a quizzical sort of scowl.

'We have another claimant for the young man of mystery,' he said, with some irony. 'Do you feel like seeing another father, looking for a missing son?'

'It isn't that other guy–?'

'It isn't,' said Bannon, 'and this one has pictures that – well, they could be you, or almost any other boy your age and colouring. You're not exactly photogenic. He also has some school yearbooks, samples of your handwriting, birth certificate and the like. Want to see him?'

'I guess so,' I said, trying to control another brief flurry of panic. 'Who does this one say I am?'

Dr Bannon turned away. 'He's a Dr Cowan,' he said. 'He's from Berkeley, California. And' – he stuck his head back through the door – 'he says your name is Barry too.'

That was enough to start the panic going again, but I suppose by now the sedative must have been working, for there was no violent heart-pounding or dryness of mouth. I lay looking at the door of the room, ready for anything.

Bannon came back, saying, 'This way, Dr Cowan.' He held the door, letting a tall, slender, slightly stooped man into the room. The man straightened up, turned, squared his shoulders as if prepared for disappointment – then drew a long, quiet sigh.

'Thank God,' he said, not to me or to anyone in the room.

And – to my utter relief – I felt none of that familiarity I had sensed about Roland. This time I was positive I had never set eyes on him before. He wasn't that Roland character – and he wasn't someone come from him to collect me for Roland. I *knew* that.

This was a good man. I could tell that. A good, sincere, worried man, and I could no more imagine him in league with that *thing* Roland than I could imagine – well, my imagination, I found out, suddenly wasn't working.

So I knew, all at once, what I had to do.

'Hello, Dad,' I said quietly. 'It's good to see you again. I guess you've heard that I've had some sort of freak accident. I don't remember much. But can we go home, right away?'

It was a fake. It didn't know him from Adam, and I felt like a lousy, rotten phony, all the while that Dr Cowan, with tears in his eyes, was showing the doctor my pictures, and promising to take me to a doctor at home for psychological tests and treatment for my head. He had even brought along a suitcase with some clothes, and he stared and frowned at the brown denim coverall, but packed it into the suitcase and urged me to put on a sweater and a pair of well-worn corduroy slacks and sneakers. They seemed to go on easily enough, though my legs stuck out about four inches between the trouser bottoms and the sneaker tops, and Dr Cowan patted me awkwardly on the shoulder and muttered, 'Good lord, how you've grown!'

He signed papers and telephoned a taxi, and before

I knew what had happened I was driving away, the hospital dropping away behind me, and every familiar thing in my life being left behind with it. I wished I could have said goodbye to Lisa. I was scared – but not half so scared as I had been in that hospital, where that Roland character might have come back the next day and demanded me!

But it was a heck of a thing to do to Dr Cowan, who still was all choked up when he spoke to me, who had shown me the woven tape with my name, so he said, Barry Francis Cowan, in the back of the worn tweed overcoat he'd brought along for me, who was urging me to look at snapshots of my mother, of a cute little ten-year-old girl he said was my sister Winifred.

'What happened, Dad? I'm still awfully confused. When did I leave Berkeley?'

'A year ago in June,' he said gravely. 'You went out to school – and none of us saw you from that day to this. We checked with the police, with the hospitals, everything–' His voice failed again, and he gripped my wrist hard, trying to smile. 'I've made four cross-country trips to look at kids in hospitals and morgues' – his voice cracked a little on that word – 'to look at kids I thought might be you. One of them was burned so badly no one could have identified him, and I was sure–' he broke off. 'Well, thank God that's all over with. Have you had supper, Barry? Does your head ache too much? Are you thirsty?' He took out a pipe, and nervously filled it. 'Your mother didn't want me to come. She's sure you were dead. She said she couldn't bear another – another disappointment. I ought to call her. Do you want to talk to her?'

'I couldn't,' I said quickly. I could stand a lot of things, but talking to the mother of this Barry Cowan, who was probably dead, and getting *her* hopes up too, was more than I thought I could take and still look myself in the eye. The silence grew so oppressive that I fumbled, 'I – I'd rather see her. How is Mother anyhow?'

'Worrying,' he said dryly, and a small frown came between his eyebrows. 'Here's the airport.' He paid the taxi and carried the small suitcase inside. 'I have a flight at nine – I would have cancelled it, of course, if you hadn't been able to leave, but if it hadn't been you I didn't want to hang around in Texas.'

'No,' I said, then, remembering that Bannon had called him Dr Cowan, decided it was time to throw in a little local colour. 'I don't suppose you want to be away from your patients too long.'

He raised his brows again, but all he said was, 'Quite right. Are you feeling all right? You look a little pale. You can sleep on the plane.'

While we waited for the flight to be called I got a good look at him. He was tall, though I realized now, not so much taller than I. I must be nearly six feet now. He had blue eyes, deep-set under thick eyebrows that made powerful ridges across his forehead; and his hair, curly and balding, was brown, salted liberally with grey. He looked alert, good-humoured, and as if, when he wasn't worried, he'd be one great father for a fellow to have. I envied this Barry Francis Cowan.

But I didn't speak until the plane was airborne and already crossing the Grand Canyon in a huge, dark chasm of black rock. Then I said, hesitantly, 'Sir–'

'What is it, Barry?'

'I'm not your son,' I blurted out. 'I *don't* remember you. I pretended I did to get away from the hospital. I'll pay you back for the flight some time – and I'm sorry I kidded you – but I'm not your son. I haven't the faintest idea *who* I am – but I don't remember you.'

He looked at me and smiled. He *smiled*.

'I knew that,' he said. 'You never called me 'Dad' in your life; you've called me 'Father' since you outgrew saying 'Papa' when you were five. You never called your mother anything but 'Nina'. My doctorate is in invertebrate biology and I'm a professor at the university – I'd be clapped in jail for looking twice at a 'patient'. Just the same, you're my son, and I can prove it to my own satisfaction, and, God willing, to yours. But not just now. Just take it easy and relax. I'm satisfied; that's all that matters.'

He closed his eyes and rested his head on the plane seat, and I blinked and stared into the darkness. Now what?

Had I jumped out of the frying pan into the fire?

Was it some sort of plot after all? How had he convinced Dr Bannon that he was my father when there was another claimant? I looked, in the darkness of the cabin, at Dr Cowan and still couldn't believe that he had anything to do with Roland.

But then – how had Roland known my name, or hit by chance on the same given name as this Cowan? Barry Cowan. *Was* it me? I didn't know.

I had nothing. My mind was as blank of memory as the dark square of the plane window was blank of scenery. Nothing – and then I thrust my hand in my pocket and my fingers closed over the shape of the little brass dragon. I must have thrust it into my pocket from the pocket of the hospital pyjamas I'd been wearing.

I had this. But did it hold the key to my lost memory – and why did it scare me so?

It was too much for me. I pushed it all aside. At least Dr Cowan was willing to wait – and that would give me time. Time to remember – or die trying!

CHAPTER THREE

The next month was, what with one thing and another, a mess.

Not that I knew it when we were coming down over the San Francisco airport. I suppose I must have thought the worst was over, when I told Dr Cowan my suspicions, and they hadn't bothered him. I'd slept during part of the flight, and had only strange, drifting dreams about nothing in particular. I awoke when the stewardess bent over me and touched my shoulder lightly.

'We're coming in over the airfield. Please fasten your seat belts.'

I tugged at mine, faintly surprised at the back of my mind that there was only one strap and one buckle to fasten. I didn't know why there should be more, but my fingers looked for them anyhow.

That wasn't a good beginning. It started me thinking about the strangeness again, and as I looked down at the lights on the field, the crawling line of lights beyond which I knew must be the freeway, the enormous coloured blinking beacons on the runways and hangars, that strangeness was redoubled. Why were we coming in at this angle? And why were the lights spread out this way? My fingers cramped, expecting to do – *something*, I couldn't tell what, and my foot moved by itself, hunting something to press, frustrated.

I muttered, 'The lights are the wrong colour.'

Dr Cowan had been dozing, but was instantly awake.

'What is it, Barry?'

I shook my head slightly, feeling my forehead draw up in a scowl. My ears ached slightly with the descent. 'I don't know,' I muttered. 'I thought, for a minute, that I remembered something. Only I guess it was just a flash of *déjà vu* or whatever they call it. That creepy feeling of – well, not exactly *I've been here before,* but *I've seen something like this and it isn't quite right somehow.*' My face wrinkled up and I felt my hands knot. 'Why in hell can't I *remember*?'

Dr Cowan's voice was calm, but I could tell he was troubled. 'Don't sweat it, son. Remember what the doctor said. Take it easy. Things will come back, and if they don't, what does it matter?'

'What does it *matter*?' I demanded, on a high note; somebody in the next seat twisted to look at me; I noticed it and lowered my voice. 'You try it. Just try it sometime and see how much it doesn't matter!' I added, harshly, 'And if one more person tells me to *take it easy* . . .'

'Look, Barry, take it – uh – relax. I know it must be rough, and sort of frightening. But it could be worse, so why not ride with it for a while?'

I shrugged and settled back in my seat. What else could I do, anyhow? Dr Cowan was being as nice about it as he could possibly be, and it couldn't have been easy for him either, if he thought I was his son, having me treat him like a perfect stranger – a nice, friendly stranger but a stranger. I quieted down, but now I'd started thinking about it all again, and I was jittering. I couldn't think of anything rougher than going into a family of strangers cold, especially where the strangers are all convinced that you're one of them and ought to care about them, and you can't prove anything one way or another.

Yes, I *could* think of something rougher.

The guy who called himself Roland. I could have been talked or bullied into going off with him – and who knows where I'd have been by now? Probably nowhere on Earth. Dr Cowan had come along just in time to save me from that – and I was damned grateful.

But grateful was all I was. I didn't feel the way I ought to feel if he were my father. Or did I? I still kept expecting that if and when I met somebody I really *knew*, my memory would come back – and when I met Dr Cowan it hadn't. Did that prove anything?

And if I was Barry Cowan, why had that Roland character *tried* to identify me? Having seen real, even if – I was sure – misguided, fatherly affection in Dr Cowan, you couldn't kid me that was what Roland felt for me. Or for anyone. If he'd ever been *anyone's* father. Or *had* a father!

Dr Cowan gathered together his bags and shepherded me off the plane. He had telephoned my mother – I called her that for convenience's sake in my mind – from Texas, but now he made another move towards a phone booth, and I glanced at the thick milling crowd. *I ought to disappear right now*, I thought. Just drift. *I'm out of Roland's reach, and why bring trouble on Dr Cowan?* But Dr Cowan looked around at me, a little apprehensively, and I realized I couldn't do that to him. He shouldn't have to lose his son after finding him. If I wasn't his son, he'd find it out sooner or later, and that would be another story.

He stepped into a gift shop. 'I thought I'd pick up some chocolates for your mother,' he said. Then, grinning, 'Still like caramels?'

I shrugged, sorry to be unresponsive. 'How should I know?'

He laughed softly, picked up the box and handed it to me. 'I'll take a chance on it.'

I didn't recognize the car either, though there was no special reason I should; it was just like thirty million other cars on the road, neither very new nor very old. I got in, opening the caramels to have something to do. I ate one. It tasted good. Of course. Why had I thought it might not? I saw him glance at me and laughed. 'It beats yeast bars, anyhow.'

He looked amused now. 'Don't tell me you've been going in for health foods! Have you taken up Yoga too?' I laughed too and denied it, but the faint sense of strangeness remained. I was going to have to get used to everything feeling somehow wrong, it seemed.

The car swung into the stream of traffic, over the Bay Bridge, along quiet streets, climbing into the Berkeley hills. Dr Cowan was silent in the car, occupying himself with the business of driving, until he made a sharp turn into the driveway of a house, dark in the duskiness, but with lights on at a side porch; then he stopped the car and turned his head to me.

'I see Winifred is still up.' He turned to me. 'Look, Barry, I know you're confused. This might not be easy for you. But try and soft-pedal these doubts of yours, at least with your sister. She's been something of a problem all this time we thought you were dead – I sometimes think it was harder on her than on your mother or me. Remember – no, I'm sorry, I didn't mean to say it that way; it's hard for *me* to keep it in mind – but stop and think. You've been not only her big brother but her hero all her life. Nina and I are old enough to take your doubts in our stride – we don't like it, but we can handle doubts and even a little hostility if we have to. Win can't – and don't forget it!'

I felt confused and guilty. All I could do was to mumble, 'I'll do my best,' and then the porch light went on and a small woman and a little girl were tumbling down the drive. Dr Cowan's hand was firm on my shoulder for a minute, then he turned me loose to be smothered.

It only lasted a minute, and then the woman said tremulously, 'Come in the house where I can get a good look at you. Oh, Barry, you're so *thin* – all right, all right, I won't fuss.' But she held on to my hand all the way up the steps and into the house. She was small, brunette, with a serious face and no makeup, and her hair was in a long braid down her back. She looked awfully young to be my mother, I thought. Winifred was wide-eyed and solemn, with dark fuzzy hair feathering up from her forehead and big dark eyes. She grabbed me and I thought of a kitten trying to climb up my shirt front, but she didn't cry. She just stood there hanging on to me and shaking all over, and saying over and over again, 'You aren't dead, you aren't dead!'

I finally prised her loose a little and said, 'I'd better not be, or somebody'll get in trouble because I'm walking around instead of being decently buried!'

She giggled a little at that, and gulped a little, and then stood back and said, 'Are you really okay? Papa said you were in a hospital in Texas. Were you there all that time?'

'No, I don't think so. Somebody biffed me over the head.' I patted her shoulder kind of awkwardly. 'So if I get to acting absentminded it's because somebody knocked the sense out of me – literally. Okay?'

'Okay,' she said warily, but smiling again. She waited till I sat down, then edged up to me again and sat down on the rug, like a kitten rubbing against my shoe tops. She said primly, 'I think amnesia is very interesting. I read a book about it, but I didn't think I'd ever know anybody who had it.' Over her head I saw Dr Cowan and Nina exchange a quick grin. *She*'d be all right. I wished I could be that sure about myself.

Nina came over and parked herself on the edge of my chair. She said, 'I don't have to tell you how I feel, Barry – or do I? Because I knew you wouldn't do this to us just for nothing. When we reported you missing, back then, they kept pestering us. Had there been a fight, quarrels, teenage rebellions? I got so sick of telling them – I must have sounded awfully sickening about what a happy home we had and what a good boy you were. I don't mean you were perfect – good Lord, no – but, well, they kept reminding me about how parents never really *know* their kids. I must have sounded like some neurotic mother type, because I kept saying, no, Barry isn't perfect, but this isn't the *kind* of thing he'd do to us. He isn't sadistic. He – he *liked* us, and if he wanted to take off for parts unknown, or go join the Foreign Legion, or hitchhike to New York, or go punch cows in Alaska, he'd come *tell* us, and ask us to forward his mail!'

I found that my throat felt funny and had to make

a try or two before I said, 'I sure wouldn't have wanted to worry you, not if I was in my right mind. I don't know why I didn't get in touch with you' – I stopped, starting to say 'Mother' and then remembering what Dr Cowan had said about my always calling her Nina, and finally I didn't call her anything – 'but I don't think it was because I didn't want to. I don't remember anything about it, but if I didn't it was because I couldn't, I'm sure.'

'Enough of that, then. If you ever remember, and want to tell me, fine. If not, don't worry about it. And now – are you hungry?'

'We had supper on the plane. But could I have a glass of milk or something?'

'As if you had to ask!'

We were kidding it, trying not to overdo it. I said, 'Funny, but I forget where the kitchen is.'

'So it's time you found out again. Right through there.' She pointed. I went through the door and found myself in a kitchen panelled with wood, with yellow curtains, very smooth and white and cleaned up for the night. I hunted in a cabinet or two until I found a glass and poured myself some milk. Inside, I heard them talking and wished I had the nerve to tiptoe back and listen in on what they were saying. Instead, I made some noise falling over my own feet before I came back with the glass in my hand. Dr Cowan, hanging my coat in a closet, turned to me and said, 'I was just telling Nina that you've grown about three inches. You'll have to get a whole new outfit – I don't think you've got a stitch of clothes that really fits you any more.'

I was a little relieved when everybody decided it was time for bed; but when I was left alone in the room they said was mine I found myself prowling around in it restlessly. All these things – the sweaters in the drawers, the old map of San Francisco and the picture of a windjammer on the wall, the shelf of textbooks and battered kid's books and sea stories over the desk, the basketball shoes and track suit hanging in the closet, these were all vague clues to the person that had been me – or Barry Cowan. But were they mine, or was I an intruder, an impostor with no right to them? I put on faded pyjamas much too short for me, and lay down on top of the bedspread, which had a pattern of anchors and sailing boats woven into it. It didn't take Sherlock Holmes to figure out that the Barry Cowan of a year ago had liked ships and sailing.

I tried to follow that one out. Had I run away to sea? I scowled, and then heard in vague memory someone calling out, 'All aboard – lock those hatches!' I clung to the memory, trembling with excitement, and following it up, had a shaking moment of real memory: a long, very narrow passage lined with metal. I heard the steps of Dr Cowan in the hall, and stepped out to intercept him.

'You look excited,' he said quietly. 'What is it?'

'I've remembered something,' I said. 'I think I was on a submarine at least part of that time.'

'A *submarine*?' He sounded incredulous. 'Do you mean you think you joined the Navy?'

My enthusiasm was suddenly quenched. 'No,' I muttered, 'Dr Bannon said he'd checked my fingerprints. I evidently hadn't been in military service.' It was a whale of a letdown. Suddenly I was very tired. I don't remember what I said to him. I went back and crawled into bed. But I lay awake for a long time, jittery with anxiety about this family I liked but couldn't feel that I belonged to – and with fear that if I shut my eyes I would wake up screaming the way I'd kept doing in the hospital. That would have been a heck of a thing to do to nice people like this.

Finally I must have slept, though, because one time when I shut my eyes, I opened them again to bright sunlight and the good smell of coffee coming up the stairwell. When I went downstairs Nina was alone in the kitchen.

'Pancakes?' She was very casual. 'Your father's gone to his office; he said if you wanted him you could telephone. Win's gone to school already. Sit down – no, get yourself a plate first.'

I found myself wanting to reassure her. 'Thanks, the food in the hospital was pretty blah.'

'Strictly speaking you ought to call the school, but we decided you shouldn't go back to school until you've been looked over by a doctor.'

I started to protest, then remembered I still had bandages on my head and leg, and burns. Time enough to worry about what they called 'picking up the threads where I'd left off'. I knew I couldn't do that, but I was willing to go along with them. There was nothing better to do.

There's no point in going into details of how I went with Dr Cowan and bought some clothes that fitted me, or how a doctor X-rayed my head again and scraped samples from the burns on my leg (I'd rather not even *think* about that, because it was fairly grim) and ran all over me with a Geiger counter. There was a big family conference including my grandfather (he was a nice, white-haired old man with a grey short curly beard, who taught cello in the university music department, but he doesn't come into this story anywhere else) about what to do about my schooling.

I'd missed a year; should I go back? My father held out that I ought to go back right away, that regular routine and old friends would do their best for me. I didn't want to make any plans until I felt a lot surer about who I was and what kind of person I had been – not to mention what kind of person I was now. Nina suggested a new school or a private tutor. Finally we compromised, which means we shelved the whole thing until January anyway. I pointed out that I was eighteen, which meant the truant officer wouldn't be coming around chasing me, and there was no awful hurry, and they let it go at that.

Things were awkward as hell; there was no getting around that. They wanted me to see old friends. I knew I couldn't hide in the house forever, but I didn't like the idea of trying to make conversation with a gang of total strangers. One came, though, trying to talk about basketball, and apparently wondering if I'd spent last year stashed away in an insane asylum somewhere, and after that Nina didn't insist any more. So I more or less spent my time with them and Winifred. I read a lot, trying to pick up the things I used to know.

But a few damned funny things happened.

For instance.

There was the night that Jens Swenson came to dinner.

He was evidently an old friend of the family. I liked him right away; a short, baldish little guy with a permanent pipe in his mouth, a face made out of pleated leather as if he'd spent all his time aboard the quarterdeck of a windjammer, and, according to my parents, thirty-two science-fiction novels to his credit. I had a short shelf of them in my room, signed by him. I don't know what Father and Nina had told him about me, but he didn't pester me with questions, and after twenty minutes' conversation I felt as if I'd known him all my life. Of course, I had, but he was the first person I'd felt that way about.

After dinner, when we were sitting in front of the fireplace, watching the driftwood fire blaze up, he fell silent, scowling into the flames, a beer can in his hand.

'What's biting you, Jens?' Father asked. 'Deadline blues? A novel to finish that you're stuck on?'

'Not exactly,' he said. 'Just a problem I wrote myself into, and I haven't got the know-how to write myself out of it. And I don't know anyone well enough to ask.' He set down the beer. 'A spaceship travelling at half the speed of light on planetary drive, and three times the speed of light on hyperdrive, expected to call in at three widely separated stars – and I can't figure out how long they'd be in space each way, or how long before landing they'd have to come out of drive to keep from crash-landing.'

Nina laughed. 'Write around that one,' she said. 'Just invent any kind of drive you want to, and keep them in space just long enough for your hero to lick your villain.'

'No,' he said, 'I'm intrigued by the relative ideas involved, but I haven't even got enough maths to make it sound plausible, let alone really figure it out.'

I was frowning over the problem. A planetary drive of half the speed of light sounded sort of implausible, but given those figures– 'Hold on, I'll work it out, Jens,' I said, and got up to go into my father's study. 'Dad, you have an old slide rule around somewhere, don't you, along with that sextant?' I was rummaging on his desk. Nina followed me to the door, and said, 'Why Barry, I thought–' but my father put his hand on her arm. He said. 'The slide rule's in that pigeonhole with the lettering guides, Barry. Go to it.'

I grabbed up pencil and paper. 'How far apart are the stars in question, Jens?'

'Well, I picked them out on a star-map to sound good,' he said a little hesitantly, and pulled a piece of paper out of his pocket. 'I've been carrying them around just in case, but I didn't know you knew that much maths.' He handed me the paper with the figures.

I frowned over them, absorbed. 'I assume they have planets in accordance with the regular mass-distance-size laws?'

He chuckled helplessly. 'I guess so. Whatever those are. I know I'm a hell of a guy to be writing science-fiction – I usually write around the scientific stuff, like Nina suggested.'

'Well then.' I moved the slide rule, frowning a little. 'If they start from Earth, you can't turn on any faster-than-light drive inside the orbit of Saturn, or you'll crash the asteroids. Say two weeks to reach that point, then to hit your first star's fourth planet, you have to come out of drive after seven weeks, two days and twenty-two and a half hours – that's allowing for your standard time-mass drift inside hyperspace, see?'

He bent over the sheet of paper, writing down my figures. I finished the computations, then asked, 'Think that will do it?'

'It's sure going to sound damned plausible,' he said. 'It looks like you ought to be writing the science-fiction in the family, kid!' He picked up the forgotten beer can and drained it. 'Where did you get all that stuff?'

'Why, uh–' I suddenly realized that the impetus had drained out of me. 'Damned if I know,' I said weakly. 'I must have been putting it together from my school maths last year.'

'Barry,' my father said quietly, 'you have good marks, but you failed required maths, and refused to take any more courses in it. I always thought you could learn it if you tried, but you said it was too much like work and you wouldn't be bothered. I couldn't even get you to learn navigation. Where in the *hell* did you learn to figure out all that stuff like an old hand?'

I shook my head and suddenly realized I was sweating all over. 'Can I have a glass of beer?' I suddenly asked. Nina gave me one without arguing. I gulped it down, almost without tasting it.

I was – *scared*.

It had seemed so real, so sensible to me, while I was doing it. And now I realized that nobody on Earth, except maybe professional astrologers – or did I mean astronomers? – ever had to figure out that sort of thing.

Jens asked, 'What was all that about mass-time drift inside hyperspace? Is that something new they've figured out in aerospace? I admit I don't keep up with my reading in the space and aeronautics field the way I used to.'

'Well, it–' I began, then suddenly grabbed hold of myself. I'd been reading something about space travel in the news magazines lately and as far as I knew, hyperspace was just a theory. 'I don't know,' I said weakly; 'it just sounded good and authentic to take a small fixed percentage of time and space for drift.'

'Oh, I'm going to use it. It sounds convincing,' he said, and my father, picking up the slide rule I'd let drop, said quietly, 'But the mass-distance-size laws about planets are accurate enough. There *is* a law which states the distance from a sun where you'll find planets – the astronomer Herschel discovered Uranus that way, by postulating that there ought to be a planet at that distance from the sun, and hunting for it there. It looks like, somewhere, you've been picking up the rudiments of celestial navigation, Barry.'

'Maybe I went to school somewhere,' I said, almost biting my lip. 'Maybe I just saw a lot of science-fiction movies.'

Jens put his hand on my shoulder firmly, almost consolingly. 'I wouldn't worry,' he said in an offhand way. 'At least you've learned something worth learning.'

Yeah, I thought, *but what?* Learned how to compute something they haven't invented yet?

Winifred giggled. 'Hey, maybe you spent all that time on a flying saucer and the little green men taught you,' she suggested, still laughing. 'And then they used one of their super-hyper rays on you to make you forget it–'

I rounded on her, taking one fast step, feeling the blood drain from my face, 'Damn it,' I yelled, 'that's enough! Shut up! Quit picking on me! Don't *say* things like that, it's not funny–'

Nina grabbed my arm. She said sharply, 'Quiet,

Win, that wasn't very funny. Barry, she didn't mean any harm.'

Winifred's eyes were huge and startled. I muttered, the anger ebbbing away, 'I'm sorry, Win. That' – I tried to make a joke of it – 'that was just a little too close to what I was beginning to be afraid of myself.'

Jens was looking at me speculatively, but like the rest of the family, he let it drop. They were so damned tactful about it, that it almost hurt. At that particular point, I think I'd almost wanted to talk about it. My memory was gone, but at this point it had shown signs of coming back, and there must have been *something* to it. And they evidently felt it would be wrong to probe.

Maybe it would. Maybe if when I remembered something, it was going to be something as crazy as that – well, I'd been reading a few books on psychology too. Oh, the maths was accurate enough. I checked that in a textbook a couple of days later. I was dead right on the slide rule and all the computations. Somewhere in that missing year I'd learned a heck of a lot of maths: good, solid stuff. But – if I invented impossible memories out of a science-fiction movie – what in the world were those fake memories trying to cover up, and why?

That was about when the dreams began.

I didn't tell anybody about them, because I knew what they'd say – it was what I tried to tell myself. Jens's talk about planets, my freak stunt with the slide rule, and Win's damned un-funny joke about maybe I spent that time in a flying saucer, all combined to give me the damnedest set of nightmares you ever heard of.

I was in some kind of spaceship, tied into a seat,

with something rigged up behind my head so if I went to sleep and my head dropped it would ring a bell and wake me up again. I had to figure out some kind of orbit or there would be terrible trouble, and behind me some kind of lock was opening and someone, or some *thing* was coming through it . . . and at this point I would wake up, swearing or maybe screaming in my sleep.

Or I was tied down in a bunk somewhere and outside the spaceport a planet kept getting bigger and bigger and coming at us faster and faster . . .

Same drill. Screams and all.

I can't have been awfully easy to live with while this was going on. Nina even started talking again about a doctor. I held out against it, mostly because I was scared. Losing your memory is bad enough; but remembering things that just *have* to be hallucinations – I kept telling myself that as long as I knew they were hallucinations, I was okay.

If it had kept on like this, I might really have gone crazy. I'm beginning to think people don't have hallucinations because they are crazy, they go crazy because they have hallucinations and don't know what to do about them. But fortunately, the next thing that happened was something tangible. After that, I knew I wasn't crazy; some damned funny things were happening but they weren't all inside *me*. And that made all the difference.

I might not have noticed the first thing, and to this day I'm not sure. It might have been an accident. But it fitted in so well with what happened later . . .

There wasn't much for me to do these days. Among other things, I was still having to check in with a doctor every other day about those burns on my leg, which didn't seem to want to heal. So I meandered around, reading books from the library, prowling around the museum, trying to pick up things I'd forgotten. Everything I learned was new, of course, though some seemed to be newer than others.

I suppose everybody who's ever had a mental breakdown thinks, at some time or other, that somebody's following him, so I told myself not to be paranoid when I noticed the same character half a dozen times in the museum. He was probably some kook from the university, who had a passion for the medieval tapestry or something.

But then there was the time I went in the restaurant for a sandwich. It was raining like the devil and my raincoat was soaked, so I hung it on a rack near the door instead of over the back of my chair as I usually would have done. I finished my sandwich, paid the bill and went to claim the coat – and there was that same little guy, walking out the door *in my coat.*

I yelled and chased after him, but the manager grabbed me to pay the bill and I lost him.

Now don't tell me that was an accident. The little guy – I never got a good look at his face – was about five foot two, and my coat looked like Dracula's cape on him. There just isn't any absentminded professor *that* absentminded.

Nina was nice when I told her about it; I'd somehow expected her to be cross at me for having lost a perfectly good coat. But later that evening the doorbell rang, and when she went to answer it, there was nobody there – but the coat lay, a soggy mess, wadded up on the doorstep. I came and carried it to hang up, and then, when I took it by the collar to shake it out, I realized there wasn't any coat left. It had been slit at every seam, the lining cut loose, every pocket ripped open and even the stiffening inside the collar pulled out and picked to pieces.

Nina did throw a fit then, and I don't blame her. I was as baffled as she was, but I think she had a sneaking suspicion that for some completely crazy reason I'd arranged to have this done. She never said so, but she looked at me in the damnedest way. As for my father, he had two theories, which unfortunately cancelled each other out. He wavered between thinking it was some idiot prank by some school kid, which gave me a fit – I couldn't imagine anyone I knew doing anything so pointless and stupidly destructive; and if they didn't know me, how had they known where to return the coat? – or that it was some devious criminal plot and he should call the police, which gave Nina a fit. She said, and with some justice, that she'd had enough police to last her a lifetime.

I could have tipped the scales towards the police, but I didn't. And I was damned glad I'd been the one to answer the phone, later that night. I picked it up and said the automatic, polite 'Hello?' and first there was a silence during which – I don't want to exaggerate – I kept hearing someone, or something, *breathing*. Not that there's anything sinister about breathing. Everybody does it all the time, so don't ask me why it bothered me, except to wonder why somebody would call me up on the phone and breathe *at* me. Then a sort of a voice said, 'Cowan?'

'This is Barry Cowan. Did you want Professor Cowan?'

'No,' the sort of voice rasped, or husked – no, neither of those things describes it, but it *articulated*. 'Did you get your coat back?'

'Just a minute,' I said sharply. 'Who is this?'

'You're clever,' the voice went on, though it sounded more like, 'Yuuh clevuh.' 'We didn't find it. Better leave it in the place you know about, or you'll look just like that coat – only in more pieces.'

'What's that? What–'

But the phone was dead, only the dial tone's buzzing emerging from it.

I stood with it in my hand for a minute, then slowly replaced it. Nina called from the other room, 'Who is it, Barry?'

I said thoughtfully, 'Just a wrong number, I guess, They asked for – somebody I never heard of,' which was, in a way, true.

I lay awake that night again, in a cold sweat. It had been bad enough thinking I was going crazy. But now I had traded hallucinations for unpleasantly tangible realities. Something out of those lost months was reaching for me – and I didn't like the sound of it at all. That coat hadn't just been ripped. It had been picked apart and *shredded.*

The idea that if I didn't recover some mysterious 'it' for that voice, I'd look like the coat, was nothing to reassure me about the tangibility of whatever had happened to me. People didn't *do* that to other people in this corner of the world, and if I had been in a corner where they did, I wasn't anxious to renew my acquaintance with it. Or them.

Maybe I should have gone straight to my father and sent him straight to the police. But it seemed to me that he and Nina had already been through enough on my account.

And what could they have wanted, anyhow? I didn't have anything on me, when I was picked up by the hospital, except the clothes I wore, a few cents in change, and a hunk of carved brass.

I snapped on my lamp to look at it; I kept it, for some reason, in the drawer of my bedside table. During the time my burns had been healing, I'd read a few of the books lying around the house – kids' books, a lot of them, and thrillers – and of course I'd come across the old yarn about the mysterious jewel which was the eye of some Eastern idol. The poor character who got away with it was dogged by sinister Chinamen or lascars, whatever lascars were, until he died a horrible death, clutching the jewel. I felt like a fool, but I wondered if the brass dragon was some melodramatic hunk of junk like that.

I was reluctant to pick it up. I remembered that, while I was still weak in the hospital, staring at it had made me throw some kind of scene. But I had to check on it.

If this were valuable, I was one of Win's little green men! It was an ordinary hunk of brass, made of the same stuff as a door key or an ashtray. It was nicely shaped into the form of a small dragon, but the carving wasn't anything to write home about either; in fact, it wasn't carved so much as milled. It could have been one of those cheap things that say *A Present from Chinatown* and mounted on an ashtray, only it seemed the wrong sort of size for that. Its value could have been something like thirty-nine cents. So scratch the mysterious eye of the idol of the Great God Foofooroney, complete with sinister Chinamen or lascars or little green men. This piece of junk could be thrown out anytime. I started to toss it into a wastebasket, then something held my hand. No, damn it, it was the only souvenir I had of a baffling experience. Even if it was only the remnant of a shopping trip in some lost-and-forgotten equivalent of Chinatown or a distant ten-cent-store – if I'd been to Texas, I might have been *anywhere* – I'd keep it until I remembered what it was and why I'd bothered to spend my probable thirty-nine cents on the thing.

I slept that night, after a fashion, dreaming that I'd been hauled off by little green men who had me tied up by one leg and were torturing me to find out why I'd bought a brass dragon in Chinatown. Dr Fu Manchu was in the dream, too, and so was Sherlock Holmes, so I didn't bother trying to analyse the dream for remnants of subconscious memory when I woke up – especially since I'd forgotten to go and have the bandages changed on that damned burn on my leg, and I didn't need little green men to torture me over it – but I did wake up with an idea. While I was waiting for nine o'clock, so I could call the doctor and make up for the appointment I'd missed, I hauled out the set of clothes they'd found me in, in the hospital, and looked them over. I called Nina in and asked her help.

'Nina, what kind of material is this? Is it what they call denim?'

'No, denim's what they make blue jeans out of,' she informed me, scowling over it. 'It's good quality stuff, though. Not nylon, probably; too porous. Nylon clothes are sweat-boxes in hot weather, and this stuff is ventilated. Maybe it's some kind of dacron blend, or a new synthetic. It looks coarse but it's very good quality, like the stuff they make sails out of for small boats, or really good tents. I don't know.'

'Where would you go to buy something like this?' I asked.

'There you have me. I thought I knew a bit about clothes and materials, but – maybe it's Army or Navy stuff. Very good quality surplus. You might look in an Army and Navy store. Or a very good sports store. But it doesn't seem to have been made on ordinary sewing machines. Look at those seams.' She demonstrated, tugging at one. 'I can't think of any sewing machines that makes crosswise stitches like that. Maybe it's some foreign stuff, Russian or something. Maybe Swiss, they make a lot of good special mountain-climbing equipment and stuff like that, and it looks adapted to rugged weather. It's not American.' She looked disturbed. 'Did you get this while–'

'While my memory was gone? Yes,' I said, 'but that doesn't mean anything. I could have been climbing mountains in Oregon and bought it or swapped it from some European tourist, you know. Or it could be some new Army surplus stuff you just haven't seen yet.'

But when she'd gone out of the room, I did the same sort of job on those coveralls that they, whoever they were, had done on my coat. It was a good idea but it didn't get me anywhere. By the end of half an hour I was sure that nothing was hidden in that coverall, seams, pockets or padded spots.

They say if you know where something isn't, you're halfway to knowing where it is. Well, whatever *it* was, I knew where it wasn't. Now if I only knew *what* it was . . .

But that line of thought wasn't getting me anywhere, so I finally got up and called the doctor. At least he was only interested in the very tangible burns on my leg, not the unpleasantly intangible things in my brain. Although, if I thought about it enough, there was something awfully damned mysterious about those burns too. Not to mention unpleasant.

CHAPTER FOUR

The next thing that happened was in the 'unpleasantly tangible' class too; the house was searched.

It was a Saturday and for once it wasn't raining, so my father and Nina decided it would be a good weekend to drive up along the coast and see the redwoods again. I gathered it was something our family had done almost every year since I was a little kid. They'd skipped it last year while I was missing, and although I wasn't in much of a mood for travel or sightseeing, I could sympathize with their wish to take up all the family things where they left off. So I wasn't about to spoil it for them; and the funny thing was that I did, sort of, remember the scenery along that Northern California coast. The way the ocean stretched, blue and misty, from Point Reyes out towards the Farallones; the enormous towering redwoods, so high that when you looked straight up along their trunks, you got dizzy and started feeling as if you were looking *down*, into a deep well of sky . . . all this was weirdly familiar to me, and in a way, comforting. Maybe I did belong here after all. Maybe all the other things were bad dreams. Maybe during that year of God-knows-what, I'd just seen too many science-fiction movies.

We spent the night up in the Russian River district, drove all through mountains and high cliffs the next day, and arrived back in Berkeley late at night, with Winifred asleep on my shoulder. Nina went to turn on the lights in the house; I set Win on her feet and hoisted out the suitcases, while my father opened the garage door to put the car away. I was just picking up the overnight cases to take them up the walk when I heard Nina scream.

I dropped the suitcases and ran. She was standing in the middle of the living room – and the place was chaos.

Chairs overturned. Rugs turned back as if somebody had been rummaging inside them. The contents of the china closet tipped out on the dining room table and two or three good pieces of Wedgwood china broken. And so forth and so on, all over the house.

My father, standing grimly in the wreckage, said, with his lips pressed tight, that at least we had insurance against vandalism. But no amount of insurance, I knew, could make up for the fright on Nina's face, or the way she looked at me. Not as if she blamed me. I'd been in the car with them the whole time it was happening. But as if, once again, I'd brought some incredible fear into their lives. It was inexplicable, and it was all over the house. They'd even ripped up Winifred's old teddy bear, seam to seam, and strewed its stuffings all over her room. That was what got me most. She didn't cry; she put on that very grown-up little face and said oh well, she was too big to play with that old thing anyhow, but she looked so *bewildered*, it broke my heart.

My father called the police right away, of course. But he kept me out of it, and he didn't say anything about the coat; he didn't say anything about the telephone threat, either, because I hadn't told him. And, though my own room was the worst of all, nothing was missing, except the brown coveralls I'd ripped to pieces looking for – well, for something. And I wasn't even sure they were missing, because Nina might have thrown them out.

It was midnight by the time the police and the insurance people had come and gone, and Nina and my father called a halt on any further discussion and speculation. But I didn't go to sleep. I sat up in my room, biting my lip, and staring at the wall, halfway back to my first theory about the mysterious whatsit of the sinister idol.

Because *this* time, I'd had that blasted little dragon in my pocket; I'd taken it along with me to Northern California. Now they'd searched my clothes – when I didn't have it – and my house – when I did. I couldn't think of anything else I had that I hadn't had before.

I turned it over in my hand again and again. It *wasn't* valuable, damn it! It wasn't made of some strange strategic metal; it was ordinary soft brass. A pin could scratch it; I know because I tried. It had a rough place on one side as if it had been broken off something; an ashtray? There was nothing inside it – I thought of that too, and went over it with a magnifying glass, but the thing was absolutely solid, without even a hairline crack. Not even Dr Fu Manchu could have hidden anything inside it.

Blast it, was I getting *completely* paranoid? Hoodlums had been known to attack and vandalize houses, even here in the Berkeley hills, for no reason at all. Did it necessarily *have* to be connected with the year I had lost out of my life? But no matter how I reassured myself, I was still afraid to lie down and go to sleep. I don't know whether I was afraid of dreaming – or of something worse happening.

I spent most of the next day helping Nina clean up the mess. My father stayed home from his office and helped too, and he must have seen how I jumped every time the telephone rang. Finally, when Nina had broken off to make us some sandwiches he stopped putting towels back in the linen closet, and turned to me.

'Never mind those now, Barry. Come here.'

I came, without saying anything, and he looked straight into my eyes. 'I don't want to nag you, son. But you know something about this, don't you?'

'No,' I said miserably. 'No. I was just wishing I did.'

'What are you afraid of, then?'

'I–' my voice tangled itself up. Finally I got out, 'I only wish I knew.'

'Barry, if you weren't so shaken up I'd never have dreamed you had anything to do with it.'

'How could I have had anything to do with it?' I burst out. 'I was with you and Nina!' Then I bit my lip and muttered, 'Look, sir, I – I *didn't* have anything to do with it.'

'But can you give me your word that it had nothing to do with you?'

I hesitated, and he said quickly. 'I'm not blaming you. But can you give me your word – Barry, I think I'd understand, if you'd got into something, if you'd joined a gang and run out on them, and they were trying to intimidate you– I don't want to sound like the heavy father, but if you'd tell me about it I just might be able to help. I can't do a thing if you don't tell me.'

I shook my head. 'It makes some sense,' I said, 'but all I can say is what I said before. I don't remember. Honestly, I don't. I swear I don't.' I felt like crying. What kind of jerk did he think I was, to let something like this happen to my family, if I'd known what was going on?

'But you know something.' It wasn't even a question. And I couldn't say anything because what I *did* remember, or guess, or surmise, could only land me with life on the funny-farm.

He looked at me for another minute or two, then shrugged his shoulders. 'All right,' he said. 'Here comes Nina with some lunch. You might think about her a little bit; she can't take much more. No, go get your lunch,' he added a little curtly, as I bent to pick up the rest of the towels. 'I'll put those away.'

I went to take the lunch tray from Nina, but I felt rotten. I knew he didn't believe me, and it hurt. I already knew he was the kind of father I'd want to have trusting me. And Nina had been through too much already. What had I brought into their house now?

I tried not to show it, but I still jumped when the telephone rang. I certainly didn't want Nina – or worse, Win – to answer the phone and hear that sinister, unreal voice that *breathed* and made horrible threats.

They say a watched pot never boils. All that day I grabbed the phone whenever it rang, and it was never anybody except the insurance company, or someone from the university for my father, or a newspaperman asking questions, or one of Win's friends wanting her to come and watch television. But the next day I went to the doctor – the burns were finally healing, but I still had to have the dressings changed – and the minute I came back I could tell from Nina's face that something else had happened.

'Barry, you had a long-distance call while you were out.'

'Who was it?' I almost yelled.

'I don't know. Whoever it was didn't give any name, and when I said you were out, he went off the line, and the operator said that you were to call Operator Seventeen in Abilene, Texas.'

I started towards the phone without even taking off my coat. 'What the devil for?'

'He didn't say,' Nina said dryly, 'but it was probably some ghost out of that mysterious past of yours.'

I stopped dead, forgetting the phone, and stared at her. For the first time it occurred to me. Other people had thought I was malingering; was it possible that my parents thought so too? My parents?

And, right on the heels of that thought, another one: *I expect them to trust me. Does that mean that, unconsciously, I really have accepted that they are my parents? Do I really believe, by now, that I am Barry Cowan, their son?*

'I'm sorry, Barry,' Nina said a little sharply. 'Don't look at me like that. I shouldn't have said that. Only – to have thought all this time that you were dead, and then to have you come back, a grown-up stranger, with all these – these devilish things happening . . .'

I felt so helpless. I suppose I should have hugged her, or something, but I simply felt at a loss. I said at last, 'Look, Nina – Mother,' I added a little awkwardly. 'Why do you think I'm so eager about all this? I'm going crazy, too, trying to figure it out – and Texas is where they found me. If it could give me even a clue – well, part of the reason I'm worried is that I *don't* want all these things happening to you and Win, and Father.'

Her face was controlled again, and she gave me a wry little smile and a pat on the arm. 'And we don't want them happening to *you*. Go and make your phone call, then, and if it sheds any light on this wretched business, be damned sure you let me know!'

I rang the operator for Abilene, Texas, according to instructions. 'There was a long-distance call for Barry Cowan?'

'Just one moment, Mr Cowan.' There were the usual buzzings and beeps, and then I heard a faraway phone ringing. And ringing. And ringing. And then the operator's voice again, like the death knell of that particular hope. 'I'm very sorry, Mr Cowan, that line does not answer. The call must have been cancelled.'

I wanted to swear. 'Who was calling?'

'The party did not leave a nay-yum,' the operator said in a singsong.

'But you must have had the number,' I said frantically. 'Whose number is it?'

'I'm soh-ry, we cannot give out that in-for-may-shun,' she said, and disconnected abruptly, leaving me again with a dial tone and a rising frenzy of frustration. Was every door going to slam in my face? Nina, watching from the door, demanded, 'Barry, is something wrong?'

Was anything *right*? I felt like swearing again, but why take it out on Nina? 'No,' I said numbly. 'Just another practical joke or something. Nobody on the line.'

When Nina had gone about her household chores again I sat by the phone, scowling. Who could have been calling me from Texas, and why? Probably the key lay in my lost memory, in something that had happened before that curtain of fogginess came down like a guillotine between me and whatever had happened.

Roland? I thought of him with shudders; but at least he had manifested an open, not a concealed, interest in me. With sudden resolution I picked up the phone, then paused and yelled, 'Nina?'

She appeared at the kitchen door. 'Yes?'

'Do you mind if I make a long-distance phone call?'

'I guess not, though it would help if you could wait till evening when the rates go down.' But I looked so crushed that she made a dismissing gesture. 'Go ahead. We aren't that short of money, and it's worth it not to have you worrying.'

But when I had dialled the number for information, and had Abilene on the line, I realized this was a false trail. I asked for Mr Roland, and realized that I didn't know the man's christian name – or even, for certain, if he lived in Abilene or had a telephone, or if Roland was his real name. I apologized to the operator and put the phone down again. Nina, on her way upstairs, taking off the apron she wore for kitchen chores, saw my dejected face and stopped beside me, asking, 'What's the matter? No answer again?'

'I didn't know where to call.'

'Barry, you were in a hospital in Texas, weren't you? Could it have been one of the doctors there, wondering if you were all right again? And – well, doctors are busy people, that could explain why he wasn't there when you called back. If you wait, he might call again.'

That, for some reason, cheered me up. That was certainly the most logical explanation. Dr Bannon had asked me to let him know how I got on, and probably the doctor who had been dressing my burns had checked with the hospital in Abilene. I even thought, with a degree of pleasure, of the red hair and perky smile of the little nurse – Lisa something – Lisa Barnard, that was it. She had seemed really friendly, not just professionally so. I pulled the telephone towards me with a resolute air, managed to get the Hendrick Hospital in Abilene without any trouble, and had Dr Robert Bannon paged and called to the telephone.

After a short time his slow, pleasantly familiar voice came through the wires. 'Dr Bannon speaking.'

'This is Barry Cowan, Doctor. Do you remember me?'

He hesitated only a minute. 'Why, of course, the amnesia case. How are you, Barry? Has your memory come back all right?'

'Not entirely, but it was something else– Doctor, did you telephone me a short time ago?'

Now he sounded startled. 'Why, no. I'm sorry to say I hadn't even thought of you for weeks. Why?'

That was a good question, and I felt like a fool. Of course not, I wasn't his patient; why should he worry about me or even think about me again? 'Oh, just that I got a call from Abilene, and missed it, and I couldn't think of anyone else. I'm sorry to have bothered you, Dr Bannon.'

'No bother at all.' He said with quite genuine heartiness, 'Glad to hear from you, and I'm only sorry I can't help you. Who else could it have been?

Did you ever hear any more from that Mr Roland who thought you were his son?'

'I thought of him, but I don't have his address and didn't know–'

Dr Bannon said, 'I believe he gave an address to the hospital. I can get it for you, if you like. Shall I switch you to records, and have them check your file?'

I thanked him and said goodbye, and he transferred the call. In a few minutes I was in possession of an address – an innocuous number on Simmons Street – and, although there was no telephone number attached, I was sure I could get it by calling the operator again.

Now the weird part starts.

I *could not* make myself pick up that phone and ask for the number of the mysterious Roland.

I could not. I *physically* could not. Half a dozen times I told myself this was ridiculous, idiotic, and reached out my hand to the phone – and then I'd drop it, weak all over and dripping icy sweat.

What the devil was I afraid of? What could he do to me from sixteen hundred miles away? Even if he had an extensible arm like one of the monsters from Jens's science-fiction novels, it wouldn't reach *that* far!

Was I afraid that, if he answered the telephone in an unguarded moment, I would hear that strange *breathing* sound and that ghastly articulation? Was I giving myself nightmares because some hooligan had a speech impediment?

I must have sat there for the best part of two hours, and I might still be there except that the front door banged and Nina came in from shopping. 'Lunch, Barry? Did you make your call? I got some of that

Monterey cheese you like; we'll have it on toasted sandwiches. Was it the Texas doctor?'

I told her no, it wasn't, and ate lunch, trying to put it all out of my mind. Briefly I wished Texas wasn't so far from California. It might be easier to go and find that Roland character and find out just what it was about him that made me cringe. I couldn't go on jumping at shadows. I'd go nuts. I laughed out loud, so that Nina stared at me; *go* nuts? According to most people, I was nuts already!

I should have known things couldn't go on like that without reaching some sort of breaking point. Nothing goes on forever; either it stops of itself, or – something happens. Considering the state we were all in, it had to happen soon. And it did.

Since the searching of the house, my father and I made the rounds every night to make sure that all the doors and windows were locked. When I was in my room, however, it seemed so intolerably stuffy that, after turning out the lights, I threw the window open. After all, Nina could be overdoing this safety business. My bedroom was on the second floor, and nobody except a human fly could get in at the window.

I stood there looking out into the night. Far away, the Golden Gate Bridge was a delicate arch of lights, like a Christmas tree garland. Beyond the bridge, the sky was flooded with full moon, and below me the garden was dark and quiet with little leaf rustlings. I lay down, looking at the moonlit window, not at all sleepy.

It might have been the moonlight that brought back the very clear memory. It was not imagination or a dream; I was wide awake. I remembered standing in a great desert, with low thick shrubbery around me, and moonlight overhead, strange greenish moonlight – and a moon curiously *small*, curiously bright.

Where had these strange memories come from? Were they only fantasies of amnesia? It was bad enough to have a lost memory; but when I began remembering things, and knowing that they were things that *couldn't* happen – what was I to think?

That was how I knew that what followed was no nightmare. I was far too keyed up, too tense for sleep. I lay there watching the moonlight, and cudgelling my brain to try to force myself to remember, and then – something moved at the window.

I don't know to this day how he got there, but I saw him clearly outlined, head, shoulders, arms against the moonlit square of window. I reared up with a yell.

'Hey, you! What are you doing there?'

There was a huge snapping roar that seemed to fill the whole room and something whistled past my head. I leaped for the light, snapped it on; the shadowy form lurched and was gone. I ran to the window to see whether he had fallen or jumped, and beyond, in the garden, something *flapped* – something huge, ugly, horrible and dark. Sickness surged up in me, and horror; I retched, and ran for the bathroom.

I just made it.

I was still there, still heaving with that inexplicable crawling sickness, when I heard them all in the hall, and after a minute my father came into the bathroom. He didn't say a word, just wet a washcloth at the sink and handed it to me. I mopped my face, but I was dripping with cold sweat again.

'What happened, Barry?'

I could only say, 'There was something at the window–' I felt my voice shaking and failing. 'I knows it sounds crazy. Something – I thought it was a man and then I saw it wasn't; it was something, some *thing*–'

'I heard you yell,' Dr Cowan said, 'and I heard– I didn't see anything, though. Barry, this can't go on. Your mother and sister can't take it. And you–' He looked at me sympathetically, but I thought I knew what he was thinking.

'You think I ought to get out? Just pack up and leave before I cause any more trouble?'

'Good God, no!' He sounded honestly horrified. 'That never entered my head. Son, how can you say a thing like that? This is your home; we're your family! Whatever happens to you, we want to share it! But we've got to find out, whatever is going on! We've got to find out if it's real, or—'

'*If* it's real,' I said bitterly. 'You still think I'm crazy! If you'd only *seen*—'

'No,' he said. 'I admit I thought, at first, that all you'd been through had left you mentally unbalanced. Now I'm not so sure. And besides – when I heard you cry out, I went into your room first, and this was lying on the floor.' He held out his hand, a small round thing lying in it. I didn't recognize it, and said so.

'It's a cartridge case,' he said, 'from a rifle bullet. Someone shot at you.'

'But – the thing I saw–' I began to shake again.

'Son, you had a nightmare and mixed it up with what happened,' he said. 'But – there was a man there, and however he got up to that window, he was real. *Nightmares don't carry guns.*'

There was no more sleep for me that night. The

blending of memory and nightmare kept me lying awake, staring into space and racking my brain for a solution.

When morning came, I knew what I had to do. It might not be the best solution, but it was the only thing that came to me, the only thing I could think of doing at this time.

At breakfast, neither Nina nor my father mentioned the disturbance in the night; I wondered whether they were waiting for me to bring it up. But when Win had taken her schoolbooks and gone, and my father was getting his briefcase, I buttonholed him in his study.

'Father, when I first came back, you told me I had some money of my own – money I'd saved after working one summer.'

'That's right. That's why I was sure you hadn't run away on your own, you'd surely have taken that with you. It was yours, and though you'd been saving it for college, if you'd left home of your free will we'd have wanted you to have it – and you knew that.'

'I want it now,' I said, and he looked at me, startled.

'What for? It's yours, you don't have to ask, but if it's for anything ordinary, we are both morally and legally ready to pay your expenses, you know.'

'I know it,' I said, 'but this isn't ordinary. I want to go back to Texas.'

I saw the startled question in his eyes and before he could ask, I rushed on 'I'm going out of my mind, not knowing what happened! I want to backtrack – to find out where I was, what I was doing, when, where, how – to do detective work on myself!'

'Do you think you can?'

'I don't know,' I said, 'but I've got to try.'

'And suppose you never do find out?' Dr Cowan asked. 'Son, I think I know how you feel, but do you think it will do any good? I'm afraid you'll simply disappear again!' His eyes were shrewd. 'You say you want to remember, but – you *have* remembered something, haven't you?'

'That's the main thing,' I told him. 'I can't believe that what I remember is real. It seems – incredible.'

'I'm good at believing things. Why not give me a chance?'

I felt tempted; and yet – how could he believe it when I didn't believe it myself? He'd surely believe I was deluded, hallucinating. How could anyone believe these weird memories of mine – memories of spaceships, of strange views of alien worlds, of things that had the form of men and weren't – surely he'd say they were dreams. I believed they were dreams, and yet I had to know why they seemed so real to me. And if these memories were not real, what *had* I been doing? Where *had* I been? And what was that brass dragon, that I turned sick and sweating-scared at the sight of it?

'Barry, is it a girl?'

I laughed a little wryly. 'No, Dad. Whatever it was, I can promise you that. The only girl I can think of is the nurse in the hospital. She's nice, and I'd like to see her again, but – she isn't part of this, and I don't want her to be part of it.'

'And suppose you never do find out why you remember these things which you say don't make sense?'

'Then I'll have no choice. I'll come home and go to

that psychiatrist. But give me a chance to prove it to myself first.'

'That's reasonable,' he said slowly. 'When do you want to leave?'

Once he had given way, he helped. He helped me break it to Nina, and even made it sound reasonable to her. He took me to the bank to get my money and put it in traveller's cheques, and bought me a new canvas suitcase.

The hardest thing was to tell Win. I knew she'd hardly got over the shock of having me come back and knowing I didn't remember her, and now I was going again. I tried to explain, but it wasn't any good. She stood there twisting her hair and biting at the end of the braid, while her eyes got bigger and bigger and blacker and blacker.

'I'll come back, Win; I promise. Don't look like that,' I pleaded. 'I'll come back.'

'If you can,' she threw at me. 'But suppose you forget all about us again, and *can't* come back?'

There was nothing I could say to that. I tried to hug her, but she twisted away from me and ran down the hall. I felt as if I would break down and bawl like a baby.

Dr Cowan drove me to the airport, and waited with me while they called my flight; and then I was on board the plane, looking down at him through the window and wondering if I'd ever see him again. I was on my way to find the year that had been sliced out of my life – if it was my life – and I had only two clues.

Roland, coming to the hospital, had known that my name was Barry.

And in my pocket was the brass dragon.

CHAPTER FIVE

During most of the flight, I found myself furtively studying the other passengers. Enough had happened to make me almost certainly expect to be followed. And yet I saw no one whom I could surely identify; no vaguely familiar face which might have come from that mysterious memory, no little man like the one who had stolen my coat; and certainly no *thing*, like whatever it was that had nearly got in at my window. Dr Cowan had been sure that was a nightmare; I wasn't nearly as sure. He said nightmares couldn't carry guns. I wasn't so sure of that, either.

The flight from San Francisco to Dallas took three hours. The plane touched down on the airport and I was transferred, efficiently and impersonally, to a smaller plane for the flight to Abilene, which was off the main airline. This was it, I told myself; if I couldn't decide what to do before I got there, I might not have the chance.

It was mid-October, but when I stepped off the plane on to the Abilene airfield, I was struck by a wave of searingly hot, burnt-dry air. The field itself was a bare expanse of white sand, with a few trees that seemed to be gasping in the heat, carefully lined up around the passenger terminal. I hoisted my one light suitcase, wiping my forehead with my free hand.

The taxi ranks drawn up before the terminal forced a decision on me almost at once. I had no place to start, so I might as well start where memory had returned. I climbed in and demanded to be driven to Hendrick Hospital.

The hospital lobby was cool, at least, and after I convinced the girl at the desk that I wasn't checking in as a patient, she agreed to page Dr Bannon and ask if he was free to talk to me for a few minutes. After a conversation over the switchboard she informed me that if I could wait for an hour, Dr Bannon could see me in his office.

It was past three when a receptionist told me to go into Dr Bannon's office. He stood up as I came in, extending his hand.

'Hello, Barry. What brings you to this part of the world again? I'd have thought you'd have had plenty of Texas for the present,' he went on jovially, motioning me to a chair. 'What can I do for you? Has your memory come back yet?'

I was just as glad he hadn't waited for answers to his first questions, because the last one was the only one I knew how to answer. 'Only bits and pieces, and what I remember isn't very – credible.'

'Have you remembered what caused the accident?'

'No.'

Bannon leaned back. He said, 'Very probably you never will, you know. That type of head injury– I'll try not to be too technical. We doctors don't know too much about the mechanism of amnesia. But one thing is fairly common, even when memory is recovered; the memories immediately before and after the injury seem to be wiped out completely. Possibly there is some injury to brain cells which store this particular memory, so that the entire impression is effaced, not only the memory of it. If you recover memories up to within, say, seventy-two hours of the time you landed in the hospital, I wouldn't expect any more than that.'

I'd have been content with that. Mostly I wanted to know what I'd been doing during the eighteen months lost out of my life. A little matter of seventy-two hours wouldn't have bothered me.

'I must admit, though, that I'd hoped you'd have more to tell me. I was fairly curious about those burns of yours.'

'So am I. So is everybody who's seen them,' I told him. 'Doctor, are there any atomic works or radiation laboratories in this part of the country?'

He stared. 'Why didn't I think of that,' he said almost to himself. 'It never occurred to me that they could have been radiation – or X-ray – burns. Was that checked?'

'I don't know, but they went all over me with a Geiger counter. But where could I have got such a thing?' I asked him, and he scowled, thinking hard.

Finally he said, 'I don't know. There are top security air bases here; anything could be going on inside them. But don't ask me to believe that if you got into an Air Force base, at least in any part of it where you could get radiation burns, they'd beat you up and dump you on the streets of Abilene. Our Air Force just doesn't work that way. If that had been it, you'd probably still be in a military hospital.'

That made sense, of course. And yet it seemed to leave no alternative except Win's little green men and their flying saucer. I told him so, and he chuckled. 'I must say that makes better sense than any theory so far. Unless you broke into a doctor's office and meddled with the X-ray machines, and he didn't want to call the police for some unknown reason.' He shoved back his chair in a clear preliminary to dismissal. 'Well, Barry, I'm glad you're getting along so well. I wouldn't worry about it. You've come through it, whatever it was, without too much trouble. Let me know how you get along.'

'Wait,' I begged, and he turned his eyes on me, suddenly kind again.

'Does this still bother you so much?' he asked. 'I hate to suggest it to an apparently healthy teenager, but your father asked if he should take you to a psychiatrist; I said I didn't think it was necessary, but if you're in this state–'

'It's not a psychiatrist I need,' I said violently, and suddenly it poured out of me. 'It was bad enough when I thought I was cracking up. I thought, if I could only be sure of that, I'd be all right! But it's real enough so that even my family is getting scared. I've got to know exactly what happened! No, don't look like that; this is no persecution complex!'

Arrested by my words, he stopped short while I told him the story; the theft and return of my coat, the telephone calls, the house searched, the bullet fired through the window. I didn't mention the nightmares, or the *thing* that had prowled and flapped in the garden. The tangible things were enough.

'So you've decided to do some detective work,' he said slowly. 'Have you talked to the police?'

I shook my head. 'What could they do? I assume they checked up on what had happened to me.'

He nodded slowly. 'But I don't know what I can do, either, Barry. I never saw you until they brought you in unconscious.'

'Until *who* brought me in? Where did they find me, and how? And what exactly was wrong with me?' I asked abruptly, 'Did I look as if I'd been beaten up?'

He stopped to consider. 'Not exactly,' he said. 'Not in the ordinary sense of the word. More as if you'd been blackjacked or got in the way of something like a telephone pole falling on your head. There was a very faint skull fracture, you know. And there's one thing you ought to consider,' he added. 'I'm not denying what you say, but such things do occasionally produce recurrent and fairly obstinate hallucinations.'

I felt a little grim. 'Ask my mother if an hallucination ever turned a house upside-down. I doubt if even a whole crew of poltergeists could have done *that*!'

He nodded. But I could see him making mental notes. 'Do your parents know you're here?'

I told him yes, knowing that he would check on it anyway. Well, I wasn't worried about what he would find out. I asked one more question, anyway.

'It was the police who found me? Do you suppose they know anything?'

'I don't suppose they'd know much,' he said, 'but there's sure to be some record of the event. You could go and ask, if you like.'

He rose again, and although I wished I could ask more questions, I knew he was a busy man, and I wasn't even his patient any more. He shook my hand again and told me to let him know how I got along, but I was so shaken by his suggestion of recurrent hallucinations that it seemed only the humouring he might give a child or a lunatic.

When I came out in the street again, into the blast furnace of afternoon sunlight, I noticed that the gates of the hospital were filled with white-uniformed nurses. A glance at my watch told me it was four o'clock. The nurses were changing shifts now; it was just possible I would see that one particular redhead for whom I was looking. The crowd of nurses thinned out, and I had begun to turn away when, at the edge of the building, I saw a slight, red-haired girl, heading for a parking lot. She was about to get into a car; I ran towards her.

'Lisa! Lisa Barnard!'

She turned, slightly startled, evidently not recognizing me. 'Did you want something?'

'You don't remember me,' I said. 'But I remembered you. You were the first thing I had to remember!'

Her eyes suddenly warmed with recognition and mirth. 'Of course! The amnesia case,' she said. 'I never did know your name, though I read on your chart that your father had come and identified you and taken you out of the state. What are you doing here?'

'It's a long story,' I said, 'but my name is Barry. That much, at least, I'm sure about.'

'It's so hot here.' She looked at me, solicitously. 'Won't you get into my car? It's air-conditioned. Well, my father's car; he lets me drive it to work.' She unlocked the door, flipped a switch and heavenly cool air began to flow through the seat.

I got in thankfully. 'It's like being on the moon or Mars, I said. 'You spend your time dashing through almost uninhabitable terrain to get from oasis to oasis. People in Texas really need spacesuits.'

She laughed heartily. 'It is pretty badly suited to anyone except a human salamander, isn't it? Maybe men should move out and leave it to the horned toads. But tell me, Barry, what are you doing here?'

'At the moment, trying to track down what happened,' I said, and told her about Dr Bannon. She listened with warm sympathy.

'I don't see what else you could do except come here,' she said. 'I couldn't have stood it either, never knowing. Are you going to the police? Let me drive you to the station.'

I demurred, but she insisted. 'The bus service here is incredibly slow; they assume that anyone important will have a car available, and they aren't concerned with anyone else.'

While we were driving, I sat back and relaxed. It was good to be with someone familiar, who took my fears seriously, instead of thinking me an hallucinating idiot going off in all directions at once.

The police were courteous, even though I told them much less than I had told Dr Bannon; only that I was trying to retrace my steps from the amnesia. All they could tell me was in their files, and the desk sergeant brought them out to show me.

'White, male, American, found lying unconscious at the corner of Fourth and Oak Streets, taken to Hendrick Hospital, treated for shock, concussion and burns.' They also had the record of a bulletin sent out on the police wires for any missing servicemen or juveniles.

'That doesn't leave you much further ahead,' Lisa commented as we came out of the police station. 'In a word, it's what they told us at the hospital. A complete waste of time.'

'Not entirely,' I smiled at her, and fell silent; it would have been hard to tell her how much her sympathy had meant. She picked up my hand and squeezed it slightly, then coloured a little and let go.

'What are you going to do now, Barry? This seems to leave you right where you were before.'

I thought about it for a minute. 'I suppose I ought to tackle Roland,' I said slowly. 'I have an address for him from the hospital.'

'It could be a false address. If he was up to some skulduggery, I can't imagine him giving his real address,' Lisa said. 'But we can try.'

'We?'

'Yes. I'm counting myself in, Barry.'

I wasn't sure I approved. If they were starting to toss bullets around, the party was getting too rough for a girl. She seemed to follow my thoughts.

'After all, Dr Bannon and I put in a good deal of work on you, Barry. Why should it all be wasted?'

'In any case,' I said, looking at my watch, 'There isn't much I can do tonight. I don't even know where I'm going to stay. I've got to find a hotel, call my family, work out some kind of a plan for approaching Roland. I can't just walk up to him and ask why he wanted to get his hot little hands on my non-existent fortune or whatever. Do you know a good hotel?'

'There aren't many hotels,' Lisa said, 'but there are plenty of motels, and you can come and go a lot more freely from a motel anyway, without going through the lobby. Suppose I drive you to one, and you check in. After that, if you like, we can go somewhere to get something to eat and decide what to do about your friend Roland.'

'Fine,' I said, 'as long as the motel's air-conditioned. I think people here in Texas should live in domes!'

She laughed. 'It sounds like a good idea at that,' she said. 'Come on, there's a good motel, not expensive, in the south part of town.'

I checked in at the motel, which was cool and comfortable; later, Lisa and I had a steak at a place she said was good. It was. That was one thing about Texas: being right in the heart of the beef country, their steaks were great.

I stopped at a news-stand next door to the steak house after we came out. 'I want to pick up something to read,' I said. 'If I decide not to do anything tonight, I don't want to be stuck with the Gideon Bible or a twenty-year-old movie on TV.'

'Here's just the right thing for you,' Lisa said, laughing. 'A story about a man who disappeared for six months and came back and told everybody he'd been to Venus in a flying saucer– Oh, my God!'

The garishly coloured paperback dropped to the floor. I turned to stare at her, saw the newspaper headline that had caught her eye.

ABILENE SURGEON KILLED BY HIT-AND-RUN

'Someone you know, Lisa?' I bent beside her, and drew a deep breath of horror as my eyes ran quickly over the story.

'Dr Robert Bannon, resident surgeon at Hendrick Hospital, was run down and killed this afternoon at approximately 4 pm while emerging from his private office across the street from the hospital. The driver of the car, according to witnesses, crossed two lanes of traffic, came ten feet up on the pavement and deliberately ran down the doctor,

then made a turn and drove away before stunned bystanders could summon assistance . . .'

'Not an accident,' Lisa said with a gasp. 'Murder! Deliberate murder! But who on earth would want to–' Her voice broke. 'Barry, he was such a *nice* man–'

I felt almost the same way. He had been so unfailingly kind. I had him to thank that I hadn't been turned over to the tender mercies of that Roland character. And his had been the first real human touch of kindness when I had come out of the nowhere of unconsciousness. I felt almost as if I'd heard that Dr Cowan had been killed.

I paid for the paper, forgetting to get my book, and hurried Lisa away from there. I clenched my fists, and spoke between my teeth. 'If those people who are chasing me around, whoever they are – if they did this, I swear I'll get them for it, if it takes me a lifetime!'

Lisa mopped her eyes with a tissue and resolutely stopped crying. 'We've got to be sensible about this, Barry. How do we know it has anything to do with you?'

'What else could it be?' I demanded. 'Did Dr Bannon have any enemies? Was he the kind of person who gets run down by a gangster? Are there that many gangsters, anyway, in a one-horse town like this? I gather he was the sort of man everybody respected and liked. Would he be connected with *two* crazy melodramas like this?'

'There is something in that,' Lisa conceded, and gripped my hand hard enough to hurt. 'Barry, I'm afraid now! If they'd kill Dr Bannon just because you talked to him, what are they going to do when they catch up with *you*?'

I wasn't worried about myself. They could have picked me off any time. I told her so. 'But I seem to be the kiss of death– Sorry, it's just a phrase, I forgot how it sounded. I'm more scared of what they'll do to *you*, Lisa. I want you to go back home, don't even take me back to the motel, lock all your doors, call the police if you hear so much as a mouse in the walls, and forget I ever existed! It's the only safe way!'

Her eyes sparked with anger.

'What do you think I am? I don't run out my on my friends that way! Besides,' she added, while I was protestingly incoherently, 'if they've got a little list, I'm already right at the top of it. I've spent the whole afternoon with you. So if I go home alone, they can just pick me off all the easier.'

This was so true that I hardly knew what to say. At the same time, I was spoiling for action, and I couldn't do much if I had to haul Lisa around with me and protect her. I didn't have any bullet-proof vests handy, anyhow.

'I still think you're crazy,' I told her, 'but if you really want to stick around, I'll do my best for you. Only I haven't the slightest idea what I'm going to do next.'

She said, 'Maybe if I'm with you they won't dare to try anything. I'd be a witness.'

That hadn't stopped them from running down Dr Bannon in front of a whole pavement full of witnesses, but I didn't say so. I felt in my pocket idly, closed my fingers around the brass dragon.

This might be what they were after. They – whoever *they* were – might not have known my memory had not come back. If they killed Dr Bannon after I had talked to him, they must have been afraid of something I might have told him, or given to him. And what else had I?

'I think I'm going back to the motel,' I told her. 'I'll put out the light and sit in the dark, and maybe somebody will try something. You don't happen to own a gun, do you?'

She didn't. 'Nothing more lethal than a golf club, I'm afraid. But I'll sit there with you. They try hard to make things look like accidents; maybe they won't try anything we can't handle between us.'

I felt strange, constrained, when Lisa came into the motel room with me and slid out of her high-heeled shoes, saying she could walk easier without them in the dark. Before we put out the light, I showed her the little brass dragon.

'They must be after this,' I said, 'although it doesn't seem to be worth anything and I can't imagine what they want with it.'

Lisa said, 'It could be the insignia or sort of a secret token of a secret society. Like the Black Hand.'

'Sounds like something out of Fu Manchu,' I said, having already thought of that and decided it was altogether too much.

'This whole thing is like something out of Fu Manchu,' she said. 'Remember the old saying: 'eliminate the impossible – and whatever is left, however improbable must be the answer.' There doesn't seem any sensible explanation, so whatever the explanation is, it's probably wilder than we can imagine.'

Silently I said amen. I'd already racked my brain trying out all the possible and most of the impossible solutions, and none of them made any more sense than Win's little green men. I'd just have to wait and see.

But I didn't dream how close we were to the solution.

At my urging, Lisa stretched out on the bed and I curled up in the armchair, on one of the pillows she insisted on giving me. I reached out one arm and put out the light.

That night remains in my memory as a strange, eerie progression of silent hours. We didn't talk much, and time crawled by with no sound except the soft tick of my watch. Every half-hour, by prearrangement, I spoke to her to be sure that neither of us had fallen asleep.

I remember the luminous dial of my wristwatch telling me that it was twelve, twelve-thirty, and I think I dozed a little before hearing Lisa's soft voice saying, 'It's one o'clock.'

'So far, so good,' I said, almost in a whisper, 'but I wonder if anything's going to happen at all. I'm going to feel like a fool if the sun comes up and nothing's happened except losing one good night's sleep.'

'Oh, well, all in a good cause– Hush!' Lisa muttered, 'I hear something outside!'

'Somebody coming home after a late movie,' I whispered, but strained my ears to hear the faint sound; footsteps? I heard bedsprings creak softly as Lisa sat up, silently reaching for her shoes.

I listened hard. If there had been footsteps, they had passed us harmlessly. But I could not rest, even though Lisa sank back on the bed.

Minutes crawled by. Then there was a slight small sound, ever so quiet, behind us. Slowly, slowly, the window square moved, a gap widened. I threw myself at the window and grabbed.

'Let go, you fool,' said a low, furious voice. 'Let me in! I think there's a Changer around and if he gets wind of us – Barry, you idiot, don't you know me?'

I almost hesitated. There seemed to be something familiar in the voice; in any case it did not sound menacing; it was not Roland's voice, but – was it a trap?

'Get the light, Lisa.'

'No!' protested the person between my hands, twisting furiously. 'Don't put a light on! Damn it, have you lost your wits? First you disappear, no one knows where, with the key on you, and now you drag the girl into it! If you wanted to consider yourself well out of it, why in the name of the Big Eternities couldn't you *stay* out? We'd have got in touch with you in our own good time, but now, if you've drawn outsiders into this–'

I didn't know what to make of his words. I reached across Lisa and put my hand on the light; my prisoner twisted loose and grabbed my wrist.

'For the last time, *no*! I have a flashlight, if you must see!'

'Give it here, then.' I took it from his hand, fumbled in the dark for the switch, flashed it on his face.

I knew the face. It was the face of a blond boy about my own age. He was wearing a brown coverall like the one I had worn, and his face was drawn and angry.

'Barry, what's got into you? Are you out of your mind? And now you know it's me, can we have that damned light out again?'

Still confused, I snapped it off. In the sudden blind

dark I heard myself say, 'I know you. But who are you?'

I heard the newcomer draw breath. He said slowly, 'That explains it, then. The blow on your head. You've lost your memory. You don't remember – anything?'

I said, 'I remember – little bits. Odd things.'

'I don't have time to explain everything. As I said, there's a Changer around – maybe two. Barry, do you have the key? Father was afraid they would capture him, and get it; he was sure they'd never think of you, so he told me he'd put it in the pocket of your uniform. I picked up your trail–' He broke off, drew a sharp breath in the darkness, then cried out, an inarticulate shout of warning.

A blue glow blossomed at the window. I flung Lisa to the floor. Without thinking, I threw my arm across my eyes and tried to burrow my way through the floor. I heard the blond boy shouting.

Then something struck the back of my head; I heard myself shouting:

'No, Rellin!'

I fell into darkness; but as I fell, something like a burst of light flamed in my brain.

And I *remembered* . . .

Part II

CHAPTER SIX

I had got into the habit, that winter, of walking home every night. From the high school, down in central Berkeley, to our home way up in the Berkeley hills, was about two miles, mostly uphill, and it was a good way to keep my muscles hard for basketball. The basketball season was over now, but I was between girls anyhow, and it was something to do. That night I'd had to look up some things in the library; by the time I started home it was dark. I wasn't in any hurry – supper would be over by the time I got home anyhow, but Nina always kept plenty in the refrigerator. I set off for home at a good swinging pace. The buses only ran up that way every forty minutes, so there was no point hanging around on the corner for half an hour, when I could walk it almost that fast.

When I heard the yell I could hardly believe my ears. Berkeley is, or was then, a quiet college town, the sort of place where a little old lady could walk across town with a hundred dollars in her handbag and nobody would touch her except to help her across the street. So at first I thought that awful yell was somebody's tomcat out doing whatever tomcats do at night. Then it started up again, this time with an unmistakably human sound.

'Help! Help!'

It died out in a sort of gasping groan, and I started running. This part of the street was half deserted, a little stretch of woods; it was so quiet after the yell died away that I could hear leaves rustling over my own running footsteps.

There were two of them running away; I started to chase them, and nearly tripped over somebody lying on the ground. The light of a street lamp fell on the pale face and I could see blood, and right then I realized that the thugs, or whatever they were, were going to get away; this guy needed help worse than the thugs needed the police.

When I got down beside him I noticed that he was only a kid, my own age or maybe a year younger. He wasn't anybody I'd seen around school, either. He was bareheaded and blond, and there was a cut on his head and the sleeve of his shirt was ripped open. There was plenty of blood too. I don't get sick at the sight of blood like a lot of people do, but I felt sick when I looked at that arm. It was a lot too much for me to handle with Boy Scout type first aid. I got up and started heading for the police callbox a block away when he called me back, weakly.

'Please–'

I went quickly back and knelt beside him. 'Take it easy, kid; just lie still. I've got to call the cops – the ambulance. You're okay, but they've got to fix up that arm of yours.'

'No.' He struggled to get up. He made it too, sitting erect, swaying only a little. 'No police. No hospital. If you please.'

There was a faintly foreign accent in the way he formed the words. I protested: 'Look, that's a bad cut. You're bleeding all over the pavement.'

'I will be well enough. I thank you, but–' He paused evidently searching for words. 'My – my father. He is not – not well; a hospital would frighten him badly. I must go home.' He put his hand to his head, then looked at his cut sleeve. 'This is not – bad. It is only bleeding.' He reached in his pocket, took out a wadded hunk of tissue and pressed it over the cut. I offered my own handkerchief; he thanked me and tried to tie it around the arm, but couldn't quite make it. I tied it for him, and when he tried to get up on his feet, I gave him my arm. His face was as white as a corpse, but he had enough guts for two; that arm must have been giving him hell.

'Look,' I said, 'the people at the hospital will break it gently to your dad, or else they'll fix you up in the emergency room and send you home in a cab. You'd better use your head and let me call that ambulance.'

'You mean well,' he said stubbornly, 'but I must go home. Please, you must not trouble; I can manage for myself.'

He actually started to walk off, swayed a little and almost fell, recovered himself, started off again; he caught hold of a tree and braced himself on it.

I didn't realize it then, but that was Karsten all over: stubborn as seven devils. I was upset about it – I didn't want the guy dying on my hands – but at the same time you couldn't help admiring him.

I caught up with him and held him upright again. 'Okay, if you want to be pigheaded about it,' I said, 'I hope your father knows plenty about first aid – or that he'll wallop you good and call the hospital anyway. Where do you live? Let's get you there and argue afterwards.'

It turned out that his house was only a few blocks away, but it was uphill all the way, and up several flights of those funny streets we have in Berkeley, where there's no car traffic, just a footpath with flights of steps along it. The blond kid didn't complain, but he got whiter and whiter, and leaned on me a little harder every block. By the time we got there he couldn't talk, just shoved a key in my hand and gestured to me to unlock the door and help him inside.

The house was small and there was nothing unusual about it; it looked as if it had been rented furnished, because the furniture was all old and worn and beat-up. It had dark panelling and was evidently quite old, like a lot of the houses up in the hills, and there was a big expanse of dark neglected garden around it.

The boy sank into a chair, and I stood there wondering what I ought to do next, when a voice called down the hall stairs: 'Is that you, Karsten?'

The kid started to answer, but his voice was weak and wouldn't carry. I called, 'It's all right; there's been a little accident, but nothing serious.' I was lying in my teeth, but if the kid's father had a bad heart I wasn't going to be responsible for him dropping dead.

There was a sound upstairs, and a man came down the stairs, slowly, with a deliberate tread.

He looked older than you'd expect for the father of a kid Karsten's age, or at least that was how I interpreted it then. His hair was snow-white and smooth, his eyes blue, and they rested on me with distrust. He ignored me and went to Karsten.

'I am sorry, Father,' the boy said weakly. 'I had no alternative except to go to a hospital. I know how you feel about my bringing a stranger–' He trailed off into some foreign language; it might have been Russian or Scandinavian. Or maybe it was because they were blond that I thought so; for all I could make out, it could have been Sanskrit or Tibetan.

I felt like a damned fool standing there. Was this all the thanks I got for hauling the kid home? I said politely, 'I apologize for intruding. Shall I go now?'

The man turned to me, and his tone was contrite to the point of courtliness. 'Forgive me. I had no intention of seeming rude; you have saved my son's life.' He bowed. 'Excuse me, I must go and fetch medicines.'

He left the room and the blond kid stretched out his hand to me. He said, 'Don't be angry with my father; he was worried about me; that is all. Don't go away.'

I stayed. It was a screwy set-up. Was the man some kind of ambassador? But what kind of ambassador didn't like strangers? Well, I wasn't too crazy about them either, so far. I made up my mind that as soon as the man came back, I'd apologize and hit the road. This good Samaritan business had its limits.

The white-haired man came back with a flat box. 'You will hold the light close, please,' he said, in the voice of a man who was accustomed to being obeyed, and handed me an extension cord with a strong light, like a tensor lamp, at the end of it. I took it and moved closer. He opened the box, and I realized why Karsten had refused to go to the hospital; his father was evidently a doctor. I held the light while the white-haired man sponged, stitched, sprayed and bandaged, and finally told me to put the light down.

'I have not thanked you,' he said. 'I thought it most important to deal with my son's wounds. I am in your debt. My name is Varzil; my son you know. You are–?'

'My name is Barry Cowan,' I said, 'and I didn't do anything; if I'd arrived five minutes earlier this might not have happened.'

'And if you had arrived five minutes later my son might have been kicked to death,' he said. 'Words fail me to thank you adequately.'

'Honestly, I didn't do anything. Now can I please call my parents? They're going to be thinking I'm the one lying dead in the street,' I said, realizing it was almost eleven at night. They wouldn't really worry unless I was out after midnight without calling, but I'd get a lecture from Nina about courtesy and not letting people worry, and I hated that sort of thing.

'I am very sorry,' Varzil said. 'We have no telephone instrument. But I dislike to see you travelling the dangerous streets alone!'

I laughed. 'Oh, lightning never strikes twice in the same place; I always go around alone. But seriously, you ought to call the police; those chaps who knifed your son might kill somebody next time.'

'I will deal with it,' Varzil said stiffly. I wondered what kind of name that was, anyhow. 'My servants will be returning in half an hour; they will escort you home in an automobile, if you can wait. Meanwhile, my son is hurt and should replenish his energies, and supper awaits us; will you join us?'

'Please do,' the boy said. He looked much more chipper with his cuts sewed up and bandaged, and he smiled at me. 'I hate to let you go like this. You saved my life, after all! What is your name? Barry? Please stay, Barry.'

I didn't stop to think more than a minute. I was hungry. I couldn't walk home in much less than half an hour anyway. If I could get a ride home, I might as well stay and have supper. So I said, 'Thanks, that would be fine,' and sat down, as he indicated, while Varzil disappeared into the kitchen and came back with a laden tray.

The food was good, and there was nothing very unusual about it; I guessed they had a Japanese cook or something, since there were things like bean curd and noodles, and the food was fixed rather oddly, but it was good and there was nothing really weird. Karsten ate with one hand, and his father sat by and helped him; I could tell that he was worried and anxious, though trying to hide it.

There wasn't much strange about the room, except for a book that lay open on the table near me; it had an illustration that looked like a spiral nebula, and the text looked like Arabic or Sanskrit. I asked, 'Are you an astronomer, sir?'

'I am,' Varzil said. 'I made that photograph.'

'Wow!' I looked closer. It had evidently been taken through an enormous telescope. 'Are you with the university here in Berkeley, sir?'

'I am sorry; I have not that honour. May I offer you more wine?'

I hadn't touched what he'd given me, and the boy Karsten laughed. 'I told you, Father, here the boys don't drink wine; get him some milk, why don't you?'

He said pleasantly, 'Perhaps you too, Karsten, should not drink until we are sure there will be no fever in your wounds; we have milk and fruit juice both.'

He went to fetch it, and Karsten said, his mouth half full of noodles, 'When I came here I found it hard to realize that grown-up people drink milk. Of course it's cow's milk, which is a little different.'

‘Where do you come from?’ I asked, and Karsten gave a quick look around. He said, ‘You probably wouldn’t recognize the name of my country; it’s not one that’s very important in America. Oh, here’s Father; do you want milk or would you rather have some fruit juice?’

I took the juice, which was perfectly ordinary pineapple juice out of a can. I glanced at my watch; it was after twelve. Karsten saw the look, and said, a little anxiously, ‘Harret should be back by now, Father; what can be keeping him?’

‘I thought I heard him in the back, but it must have been something else,’ Varzil replied. ‘Let me go and see. He might have gone directly to his room, not thinking we would want him at this hour. I will–’

He broke off, with a smothered exclamation in some other language. Then he whirled round to us, suddenly active as a cat.

‘Karsten! Get down! There’s a Changer around,’ he said, and gestured me imperiously back towards the corner of the room. He leaped for the light, snapped it out, and I heard a drawer rasp in and out. A dim blue light sprang up from nowhere, and in the glow I saw Varzil’s hand and arm holding a slender blue-glowing glass rod.

I pressed myself against the wall, feeling as if I’d suddenly walked into a gangster movie.

Karsten slid noiselessly off the sofa and rolled towards the corner of the room. The blue glow filled the window. For a moment a great dark shape rose there, grew, moved and altered monstrously; a broad, flat, reptilian head flickered against the shadows. I passed my hand over my eyes; I was seeing things!

I *was* seeing things; the form at the window was a man's form, dark and squat, weapon in hand, shouting. Varzil edged back, wheeling his weapon, whatever it was. Then the moment of stasis broke. Karsten yelled, 'Harret! In here!' There was the sound of swiftly running feet, the door burst open and light exploded in the room.

Varzil fired twice with the blue rod; it made a hissing crackling sound. There was a strange receding howl. Then the blue glow at the window died and the garden was dark and empty again.

Varzil went and picked up Karsten from the floor and put him on the sofa. There was another man in the room now, tall, white-haired like Varzil, but infinitely younger; Varzil went to him and they conferred briefly in that mysterious language. I moved. I felt stiff, shaky and very much bewildered. I went over to Karsten and asked if he'd hurt himself; he said no, but I could see that the knifed arm was paining him. I kept wondering what the devil I had walked into. And at the back of my mind, quite incongruous with all that was happening, I was wondering when I was going to get home tonight.

To say I knew, then, that I'd walked into something fishy, would be an understatement. I'd known that for some time now. But my first thought, that I'd somehow got caught in the crossfire of gangsters, had given way to a strange, half-panicked, half-excited Wild Surmise. That strange weapon of Varzil's, and above all the incredible dragon-shaped head at the window, made me realize I had stumbled into something *very* strange and uncanny. Part of me wanted to hightail it out of there, before they remembered the innocent bystander in all this. But part of me wanted to hang around and see what in the world was going to happen next.

That's me all over. Barry Cowan, damned fool. If I'd had the brains, I probably could have got out while Varzil and the newcomer were still excitedly comparing notes, and the chances are they wouldn't have thought about me again.

Before long I realized they'd remembered me. Karsten broke in, speaking English again.

'You can't do that, Father; he saved my life, and it would be wrong, wrong, *wrong* to drag him into this!'

Varzil said slowly, 'you are right, Karsten, speaking from the point of view of pure ethics. But practically, we cannot take the risk. We must bring him along, and take the responsibility with the–' He used a word I couldn't understand; it sounded like *Congo*, which made no sense at all in that context.

I thought it was time I spoke up for myself. I said, 'I think I'd better be going.'

I think I knew already they weren't going to let me go.

Varzil lowered his head, looking away from me. 'I am infinitely sorry,' he said. 'I fear we cannot let you go just now.'

The hell of it was, he really did sound sorry. He went on to say, 'This is a poor reward for your kindness, but I very much fear you must come with us.'

The newcomer in the room was moving around, putting a few papers into what looked like an ordinary collapsible briefcase; he dashed up the stairs, came back with an armful of something else and stuffed that in too. Karsten got up shakily, and came towards me.

He said, 'I'm sorry about this; I swear I am. I tried to tell them–'

I felt almost too bewildered to be frightened.

'I don't understand,' I said. And, boy, was *that* an understatement. 'Why should I have to go anywhere with you? What has all this to do with me?'

'We are leaving,' said Varzil slowly. 'The rendezvous is within fifteen hours. I dare not take the risk that you will talk about this with your people. I must take you along with us. Do not be afraid; you will be released, unharmed, when it is safe for us.'

I felt awfully futile as I said, 'I wouldn't tell anybody anything. Who would I tell?'

'I am sure you could trust him,' Karsten said eagerly, and Varzil seemed to hesitate, then shook his head.

'I might trust you,' he said slowly, 'but I dare not risk the possibility that something might slip out, unintentionally. This is far too important to take any risks.'

I burst out, 'So this is what I get for trying to keep your father from worrying! My own family is going to be damned scared when I don't come home!'

Karsten looked away from me; his face was red.

Varzil repeated slowly: 'I have told you; I deeply regret this. If there was any alternative, I would not insist.' He glanced at the man who was packing the briefcase.

'Harret, are your preparations concluded?'

'We can leave at any moment,' Harret said. His accent was thicker than Varzil's and Karsten's.

Varzil got a thick duffel coat from a closet and put it on Karsten; he enveloped himself in a similar garment. Karsten winced as the coat was buttoned over his arm, tried to grin. 'Oh, well, at least this is the last time I'll have to wear these absurd things!'

Varzil came towards me, carrying what looked like a sailor's pea jacket. He said, 'Your clothing is thin; you had better put this on; it will be very cold.'

That was when I exploded. I yelled, 'I'm not going anywhere with you – and you can't make me!' I made a break for the door.

I'm a basketball player, tall, and strong, and muscled pretty well for my size. I figured I could knock the old guy out of my way and outrun any two of them. It was a heck of a way to treat a nice old man, but he'd asked for it. I braced myself–

And I got the shock of my life.

The old man must have been made of best quality sprung steel! He was strong, so strong that he literally picked me up as if I'd been a four-year-old child, and pinioned my arms at my side. I kicked hard, forgetting about the rules of fair play, and hammered at his face, and he didn't pay any more attention than if it'd been a little kid having a tantrum. He held me that way, not moving, not paying the slightest attention to all my squirming, kicking and yelling. Varzil just stood there, smiling gently and regretfully.

'I am sorry,' he repeated. 'I would not like to coerce you. I would much rather you would come with dignity and patience. You have been a good friend to us and I wish you would be co-operative. I give you my word, the word of a Commissioner' – I'm almost sure he said *commissioner* – 'that you will not be harmed in any way, and that you will be released at the first opportunity.'

What could I do? I was held as firmly as if a huge octopus had wrapped itself around me. Wherever they were going, it looked as if I was going with them. I couldn't do anything, and they didn't sound as if they intended to hurt me. After all, anyone as strong as Varzil could just as easily have knocked me over the head and I wouldn't have given him half as much trouble.

I said, 'When kidnapping's inevitable, I might as well relax and enjoy it. All right, you needn't tie me up; you've made your point. I'll come along.'

Varzil set me on my feet. He wasn't even breathing hard. He said, 'It will be cold. I beg of you to put on the heavy coat. It is my son's, and I assure you it is clean and sanitary.'

I almost laughed at that, as I put my arms into the coat. Karsten was shorter than I, but he was stockier so that it was a fair fit; and it certainly was warm. A lot too warm for a May night in California; it felt as if it had been intended for mid-winter in Siberia!

He seemed to know what I was thinking. 'I assure you, you will be glad of it before this night is over. Come with us now. I implore you to be quiet, not to get sudden ideas about shouting for help; this house is very isolated. You will not be hurt. Harret, you have all of the special films? The two smaller–' It sounded like *thingtangles*. 'I think we may safely abandon the larger one.'

'Everything is ready,' Harret assured him.

Varzil motioned me to go before him. He supported Karsten with his arm. Harret led the way out to a dark back yard, thickly grown over with rhododendron and tangled undergrowth. Harret flashed a small pencil of light at our feet, allowing us to keep from stumbling over rocks and roots. Karsten stumbled anyway, and Varzil, with a few soothing words in the strange language, picked him up and carried him. Good lord, the man was strong! No wonder Karsten hadn't made more fuss over a knifing that would have put me in the hospital for three weeks!

What on earth were these people, anyway?

We ended up at the dark, ivy-grown wall of what looked like an old garage. Varzil set Karsten on his feet and signalled to Harret to hold the small pencil light close.

There was a tangle of formidable padlocks and chains around the door. Varzil took out a bunch of keys and worked over them until at last he could shove them all aside and open the door; then he stepped back to allow Harret, supporting Karsten, and me, to enter the darkness. I had to drag my feet; they didn't want to move in that darkness. Behind me, Varzil slipped through and, by the pencil light, manipulated the locks again. Then he spoke briefly to Harret, a switch moved, and there was light.

And I nearly fell over backwards, except that Harret was crowded up against me.

Right ahead of me, in that dusty garage, filled around the edges with the junk of a dozen other tenants, pitilessly outlined in the new harsh light, *it* stood.

In this day and age nobody, but nobody, could mistake the outline of a flying saucer.

CHAPTER SEVEN

I think I must have been paralysed for a few minutes. I have no idea what I did next. I don't think I said anything. It went too deep for that. I guess I simply didn't believe the thing was real.

It didn't look like the ones on the TV programmes, of course. It was about fourteen feet across, I guess, and instead of being metallic, it was painted an almost fluorescent blue. It had the standard outer ring and dome in the centre. I was dumbstruck for a few minutes; then Varzil shoved me very gently towards some sort of steps that went up into the thing. I realized I was expected to go up in there.

When something like that happens you don't believe it. At least, I didn't. But when I set my foot on the first step, something snapped inside me. This *wasn't* a gag or a crazy nightmare. I felt a thickness surging up inside my throat, and wanted to scream. I was awake, and this was *happening*! Furthermore, Karsten was climbing into it as if it were a Number 7 bus! His calmness made the wheels of my brain start going around again; from feeling as if I were trapped in a nightmare I began feeling as if this were simply some very strange, but quite explicable situation. Evidently they were spies, possibly Russian. Heaven only knew what the Russians were doing these days behind the Iron Curtain. In any case, I couldn't do anything, so I had better go along, keeping my eyes wide open and my mind alert.

I felt calm again, a funny iced-over calm. I stepped into the saucer. It was fixed up inside like a carnival ride, with the seats and belts and braces, padded so that people wouldn't slide around in the seats. There was machinery at a panel inside, vaguely like the control panel of an aeroplane. I couldn't make head or tail of it. Varzil settled me into a seat.

I finally found my voice.

'Where are you taking me?' I demanded. 'Russia?'

Varzil sat down in his seat, moving the padded braces around him, sliding his knees into the rests, with easy competence. He said, 'No, not Russia. We have no interest in your country's secrets nor any other country's; we are not like the–' It sounded like *deekri*. 'I am a scientist. We are forbidden to interfere in the internal affairs of this world. That is how you may know you are safe; even if you wished, it would be quite forbidden for us to take you out of your own solar system. You will be returned on a shuttle ship within a few hours.'

Once again I had that you've-got-to-be-kidding, empty sensation in the pit of my stomach. *The solar system!*

I said rudely, fighting the surge of panic and disbelief, 'Don't try to tell me you're a man from Mars!'

'No,' Varzil said, quietly and matter-of-factly. 'Mars is only marginally fit for human habitation, although the *deekri*' – that word again! – 'survive there quite well. We usually avoid Mars when we can, although it is used as a scientific base for explorations in this system. No, our home world is entirely beyond your sun, but you will be returned before we leave this system.' He bent over the control panel. 'I am sorry, I cannot answer more of your questions now; I must check my timing.'

I sat back in the softly padded material of the seat, a strange taste in my mouth. I hardly recognized the taste of fear. Flying saucers parked in a garage! Aliens from the stars renting a house in Berkeley! Surreptitiously I pinched myself. It hurt.

Somehow, the garage roof slid back. Don't ask me how they engineered it. Lights glowed in all colours around us, red, blue, green, amber, back to red again. I braced myself as a very soft humming noise began. Karsten reached a hand to me and said, 'Don't be frightened; the acceleration in the shuttle ships is not at all dangerous.' Still bracing myself, I remembered the steel strength of the old man and wondered if human flesh and blood would take the kind of acceleration they called not at all dangerous. Then there was a sort of tingling through the whole framework; the coloured lights flickered faster, wavering over our faces as the humming rose to an eerie high-pitched whine. I realized we were rising, slowly, then faster and faster.

The high-pitched whine gradually climbed up and up through the audible range. The lights moved through the range of colours and back again. Varzil was moving his hands slowly at the controls. I felt myself crushed back against the seat as the whine died into noiselessness; the pressure grew and grew. There was a very soft hissing noise in the cushion behind my head, and I smelled the unmistakable sharp tang of pure oxygen.

The pressure lightened and was gone. The shifting spectrum of colours steadied, evened to a smooth, pale blue light, like a fluorescent bulb. Our faces were a ghastly colour, but everything could be seen with perfect clarity. Varzil loosened his safety straps and leaned back in his seat. He motioned to Karsten, who was unfastening his own and then stood up and came over to me.

He said, 'The shuttle is locked on automatic control now, and acceleration is finished. Now I am free to answer your questions, if you wish. There may be some things I cannot answer, but in so far as I am free, I am at your service.'

I said, trying to keep my voice from trembling, 'If you wouldn't let me loose to talk about the characters who broke in on you, am I supposed to believe that you're going to take me back to – to Earth to talk about *this*?'

Varzil smiled and looked apologetic. 'About this you may talk freely, if you can gain any audience,' he said. 'There is now no proof available to you. If we had released you before we left, someone might have prevented us from leaving.'

That, I realized, made a certain sort of sense. I had laughed at enough flying saucer yarns myself. Who would believe this? I could just see myself trying to convince Father and Nina – let alone a couple of tough cops – that I'd been kidnapped for a ride in a flying saucer.

But meanwhile, I was bursting with curiosity.

'Just where do you people come from? Where are you going? What were you doing in Berkeley?'

Varzil hesitated. Karsten said quietly, 'There is no reason not to tell you. My father is the representative of the Council of Worlds – our home is on the planet of the star you call Spica. He came here to study astronomy from this part of the galaxy. As you know, your world is in an isolated arm of the galaxy, and some views are easier to get from a less populated part of interstellar space. We have another commission, too. It would mean little to you.'

'And where are we going now?' I asked. I felt vaguely proud of myself. Galaxies. Planet of Spica. Here for astronomical study. Oh, sure, nothing to it, happens every day.

It was Varzil who answered. 'In eleven hours we will rendezvous with our mother ship, which is in orbit outside of your moon. After this, you may be taken back and released. I suggest you settle back and enjoy the trip. You are well clothed, so you will not suffer from cold.'

Strange as it seemed, I decided to do just that. There was nothing else I could do. We were out in space – unless this was an incredibly elaborate hoax. Karsten was already pulling his thick coat up around his ears and snuggling back into the soft seat.

Varzil bent to check an instrument panel again, saying offhandedly, 'Navigation out here is nothing; closer to the surface of your world, of course, your skies are so cluttered with satellites that we must keep out of their way.'

I asked, 'Do many of your saucers – shuttle ships, whatever you call them – come in and out? Why has nobody ever tracked you on radar?'

'Radar? Oh, yes. The material this ship is made of is impervious to your devices,' Varzil said. He shivered, and suddenly I realized that I, too, was very cold. He said, 'For such short trips it is not feasible to use solar engines for heating, but your coat is warm. Look, my son is asleep. I suggest you sleep too; it is very late.'

He bent over the panels again as if he were tired of

talking. I lay back against the cushion of the seat. My watch read past four, and I realized I was very tired. I lay watching Varzil, who sat very still, his white hair fluorescing vaguely in the blue light. As an adventure, I decided, this was definitely a bust. I couldn't see anything and nothing was going on.

Strange as it seemed, I must have fallen asleep, because when I opened my eyes again, Varzil was asleep in another seat and Harret was at the controls.

It went on like that for hours. Dozing, waking, sleeping again. Once, Harret produced a meal of sorts. I grinned a little wryly, because it looked and tasted just like surplus Army C-ration, and I found out afterwards that was exactly what it was. They had discovered it made excellent, long-keeping emergency rations on board the shuttle ships. But at the time I wondered why the hell a galactic civilization couldn't have invented some better kind of food.

Varzil looked at Karsten's bandages, and checked a burn on Harret's arm, which had resulted from the skirmish back in Berkeley. I didn't ask any more questions and they didn't volunteer any more information.

That doesn't mean I wasn't *thinking* plenty. Why the sudden departure act? Had Karsten really been mugged by local hooligans, or was this part of their Galactic Spies act? If they were here only to study the stars, why should they be attacked with weapons which left nasty-looking burns?

Karsten woke up again, took a packet of the C-ration stuff and chewed on it. When he finished, he looked friskier than I'd seen him yet, and he came to sit next to me.

'This is a wretched thing for you to get into,' he said. 'I hope no one will be waiting for you and worrying!'

I'd been trying not to think about that. Nina was going to be worrying herself sick. And, when and if I did get home, what *was* I going to tell them, anyway? I said, 'My mother is going to be scared.'

Karsten said, 'My mother died when I was very small. But I think I know how you must feel.'

'It isn't your fault,' I admitted.

'Please don't be angry with my father. He has his duties and responsibilities, you must know. He would never hurt anyone willingly.'

I said, 'is this why you wouldn't call the hospital? You were afraid they'd find out something about you?'

'Oh, no. But as I said, my father is not strong.'

I laughed, remembering the steely strength of those arms, and Karsten protested.

'No. He has a – a weakness. I feared to shock or frighten him. I knew he would be afraid I had been attacked by the *dikri*–'

I said, 'This is the third or fourth time you've mentioned them. Who or what are they?'

'They are – it is hard to explain,' Karsten said. 'They are – they come and go in the galaxy. Your planet is out of bounds without official permission, but they come and go without permission. They are – a form of outlaw. They are different; they cannot get by without strange disguises. It is hard to explain. I do not like to talk about them,' he concluded, looking slightly helpless.

Curiouser and curiouser! Not one group of aliens but two, and one of them Karsten couldn't describe!

Coming and going on Earth, for inexplicable reasons . . . Evidently the many stories of flying saucers had some foundation in fact after all! But I wasn't going to believe in Bug-Eyed Monsters!

I asked, 'How does your ship fly? Obviously it isn't rocket power, and it couldn't be atomic power or someone would have spotted the radiation in the atmosphere.'

'It uses magnetic currents and the energy from your sun – that is why it cannot be used outside the orbit of your fifth planet; the solar fields are too weak.'

Which, in effect, left me no wiser than I had been before. Who was I to imagine I could understand the science of a galactic civilization? Just accepting that there was such a thing strained me to my limits.

It was about half an hour later when Varzil raised his head from the control board; there was a worried note in his voice.

'Harret,' he said, 'come here and check my reading. I can't get anything that makes sense. Either the instrument is out of focus, or – well, or else it isn't, in which case–'

'Let us hope the instrument is in error,' said Harret a little grimly. He crossed the middle area of the compartment and leaned over Varzil's seat at the control panel. The seats were situated around the outside rim of the circular saucer; the diameter was about nine feet. Harret twiddled one of the switches. He scowled, knelt down and unfastened a shielding plate and twiddled something inside *that*, then got up and checked the reading over Varzil's shoulder again. That went on for several minutes, while Karsten anxiously watched them. I watched all three of them, thinking, *Oh, great, my first ride in a flying saucer and something goes wrong.*

Varzil finally unfastened his belt and slid out of the seat. Harret took his place, but after a minute, he, too, relinquished it, and said, 'It's no use. We're already out of orbit to the point where we aren't going to be able to rendezvous with the mother-ship.'

Karsten said, 'Father–?'

Varzil took out something like a handkerchief – only it was iridescent green, and four times as big – and mopped his forehead. He said, 'I wanted not to worry you. But either our instruments are very badly damaged – and I don't see how that could have happened, since they were in good order when we took off – or else we are in an anti-proton damping field.'

Karsten said, and it sounded like swearing: '*Dikri!*'

'I'm afraid so.'

I was fairly sure it was no time for me to butt in, but I'd sat watching this performance for some time now, and it was my skin too. I asked, 'is something wrong?'

Varzil turned to me with an impatient gesture, then controlled himself and said, 'Yes, you have a right to ask questions. Something is very much wrong. We are being drawn off our course. Karsten, will you explain to him?' He knelt down, removed another panel and started doing incomprehensible things inside it. I felt like a jaywalker on the freeway when traffic is halted in every direction and the cop starts swearing; definitely in the wrong place at the wrong time.

Karsten moved into the seat next to me. He looked badly scared. He said, 'I mentioned the *dikri* to you. It was a *dikri* who tried to break into our house last night. One of my father's tasks on your planet was to report any interference with the legitimate concerns of scientists within this solar system by the *dikri* or their kind. Of course it is to their interest to keep him from making his proper reports. We thought we had got free without having them on our trail, but there must be others in this sector. They are generating a field which prevents us from taking in solar energy – do you understand?'

'Not exactly,' I said, I seemed to be given to understatement these days.

'Well, it's like– Have you ever heard of a tractor beam? There isn't any such thing except in science-fiction, but it works the way a tractor beam would if there *was* such a thing.'

'Oh, *no*!' I put both hands to my head, wondering if I'd wandered into somebody's else nightmare, while Karsten explained earnestly.

'They get between us and our objective with this field, and we cannot take in solar energy beams to proceed in our proper direction. So, like all free-falling objects in outer space outside a planet's gravitational field, we fall into orbit around the sun, or the nearest large body – and, since that direction is easy for anyone to predict with a slide rule, we can be followed and even attacked.'

'You mean, in effect, we're drifting instead of being under control,' I said, and Karsten said, 'That's it exactly. Without solar power we are subject to the same laws as any other celestial body.'

'And,' said Varzil, 'this means that all they have to do is to get into that orbit. They do not need to draw us down to them; they need only wait and we will inevitably fall towards them.'

'And isn't there anything we can do about it?'

'Nothing, without a source of power, and inside this field we cannot take on power,' Karsten said.

Then they all started jabbering together in their own language while I thought, *Maybe these* dikri *or whatever, aren't as bad as they're painted.* Maybe they would even rescue me from these characters. They had been pretty high-handed, talking about the legitimate concerns of scientists in this solar system, meanwhile not bothering to get permission from *us*, only from some galactic government off somewhere. I wasn't so sure I liked the idea of Varzil's chaps coming and going on Earth without so much as a by-your-leave. There was no reason I should assume, automatically, that the *dikri*, whatever they were, were the villains in this Cosmic Drama I seemed to be stuck in, and Varzil and his friends were the heroes.

In the next couple of hours Harret and Varzil alternately fiddled with controls that weren't working, gave up in disgust, took out slide rules and worked them, then started messing with the controls again, the way you keep trying to start a car several times even if you suspect it's out of petrol; just in the hope your gauge is wrong. Finally they both gave up and sat down in the spare seats.

'There are times,' said Harret, 'when I am inclined to criticize the Centre for their Weapons Control law.'

'Particularly since it is unenforceable,' Varzil said bitterly, 'and disarms only the law-abiding citizen without affecting the outlaw.'

After that, they each took out a couple of the blue-glowing rods I'd seen last night, looked them over and put them aside, while Karsten explained that they did not operate outside the gravitational field of a planet. I sat there wishing my nails were long enough to bite effectively and wondering if, when these *dikri* caught up with us, I'd be rescued or murdered. We ate some more of the rations, the three aliens in the manner of condemned men enjoying their last meal. It kept getting colder and colder, and Karsten seemed uncomfortable, although he didn't complain. Then there was a curious, hard jolting sensation, the coloured lights within the saucer flickered on and off again, there was a whicking sound, and the door we'd come in by began slowly to open.

Karsten muttered, 'We must be fast to their hatch.' He was white to the lips. I found myself hanging on to my seat. And then the *dikri* came in.

He looked human: short and squat and flab-faced, but certainly not a bug-eyed monster; he had the right number of arms and legs and heads and noses and things. With both hands, he held a thing that looked like a short whip.

Varzil looked as if he was holding on to his seat too, but he kept his composure. He said, 'So it is you, Rellin. I should have known you would not accept a warning and Notice of Dismissal.'

'I did not come to make conversation,' the thing said. I said *thing* because the minute it spoke I knew it wasn't human. Something *crawled* down my spine, the way it had when I had seen that monstrous shape at the window of Karsten's living room in Berkeley.

'Varzil,' it articulated, 'and his spawn. And this one?'

'Rellin,' said Varzil harshly, 'this is an Earthman and by law a neutral!'

The *dikri* shrugged. 'Neutrals are none of my affair,' it said. 'This one is no good to me.' It raised the whip-thing. Varzil lunged, but too late. There was a greenish flare; Harret gave a strange stifled cry and fell limply out of his chair. My flesh crawled. I didn't need anyone to tell me he was dead: the thing had just shot him down without even thinking about it! I hadn't known Harret – he was less to me than Karsten and Varzil – but just the same he was an inoffensive human being, he hadn't been doing anything, he hadn't even been *resisting*, and the – the thing had just raised its weapon and wiped him out of existence!

Varzil was swearing in a choked voice. Karsten's eyes were filled with tears. The *dikri* did not even look at the dead body of Harret. He said, 'Varzil, you will come with me, or I will kill your spawn and the neutral.'

Varzil looked around helplessly. He got up out of his chair. 'What do you want with me?'

I was thinking, incredulously, *Wasn't he going to do anything?* It had shot down his friend, companion, co-worker, and was he just going to knuckle under? The *dikri* pushed Varzil roughly ahead towards the open door. Twisting a little in my seat, I saw a rough metal passageway between the saucer door, and beyond it, a blazing light which, I suspected, must come from inside the *dikri* ship. Varzil went quietly, saying only, 'Karsten, do nothing rash.'

Something boiled inside me, and I rushed in. Rellin turned its back on us for a minute to shove Varzil through the door, and I leaped.

Rellin went down under me, crying out. I kicked, and it must have hurt – because it gave a yell of rage – no, a roar, an inhuman screeching howl; it squirmed, reared up to a crouch and it–

It *changed*!

Before my eyes Rellin's face melted. That's the only way to describe it. Karsten shrieked at me in warning, but I was already backing away. It had dropped the whip-thing; I kicked it, slid and tripped, my horrified eyes fastened on the incredible transformation taking place in the *dikri*. Flesh seemed to flow like water, the crouched form hunched, rippled into a greyish wrinkled clawed mass. Where a man-form had stood – a dragon roared at me.

One paw ripped out and I went rolling, feeling blood break from my cheek. Karsten grabbed up the whip-thing desperately, but the dragon flapped, lunged, and in the cramped space Karsten fell backwards over a seat, dropping the weapon. A moment later the *dikri* had snatched it up and without another glance at us, as if we were too insignificant to mention, the dragon-form thrust Varzil through the opening. The door closed behind them.

CHAPTER EIGHT

For a minute I lay where I had fallen, wondering if my eye had been ripped out; I couldn't see out of it, and I was sick all over with horror. Then I started to come to a little, and dragged myself upright. I wiped my eye and realized I could still see. Karsten still sprawled on the seat where he had fallen, and he was sobbing harshly, whether with pain or humiliation I could not tell. He looked too dazed to know what he was doing.

I looked at the closed door, still almost unable to grasp what had happened, and picked myself the rest of the way up. Varzil was gone and Harret's body lay limp and horribly dead on the floor, and Karsten still sprawled there crying.

I went over to him and saw that the bandages had come loose, and he was bleeding again. Trying not to hurt his bad arm, I tried to lift him upright. 'Stop bawling,' I said roughly. 'I'll do whatever I can for you, but crying won't help you – *or* your father.'

Refusing my arm, he pulled himself up and went to kneel by Harret's body. After a little he covered the man's face. When he turned back to me he looked grim and angry. 'He cared for me when I was a little child,' he said, 'and they killed him like an animal, without even anger against him. Should I be too unfeeling to mourn for him?'

I felt vaguely ashamed of myself. The dead man had been nothing to me, and yet the manner of his death had been shocking. Karsten certainly had a right to be upset, especially when his own father had been taken away by the same people – no – *things*. And Karsten was hurt himself. I bleakly remembered how I had hoped the newcomers would rescue me from Varzil and company.

I was beginning to feel a little less dazed. Karsten wiped his face and tried to readjust the bandages around his arm; I helped him. Then I asked, 'What – what *are* those things?'

'*Dikri*,' said Karsten. 'Shape-changers. You have, on your Earth, legends of werewolves. The dragon-shape is their true shape, but they can adjust it to pass as human among men.'

'But how can they change like that? Solid flesh and bone? Is it real, or a sort of hypnotism?'

'I don't know. I don't think they are all solid flesh and bone at all. I don't know how they change. I only know that they do.' He shuddered, bone-deep. 'I had never seen it before my eyes like this. It is horrible, horrible!'

It certainly was that. I wondered what they would do to Varzil and realized that I didn't even want to think about it. I also wondered what they would do to us, and if there was anything we could do to prevent it, whatever it might be.

Neither of us spoke for quite a while after that. Harret's dead body was not the most pleasant company, either. Karsten, poor kid, must have had even more frightening thoughts about what was happening to his father inside the *dikri* ship.

At last I said, 'Shouldn't we be deciding what we're going to do when they come back to us?'

'I don't know what we can do,' Karsten said.

'We're unarmed, and they have all the weapons they need.'

I supposed he was right. Heroism sounds good, and looks good in the movies, but deep inside I knew it wasn't going to help much to try to jump that creature in the shape of a man, unarmed. And there was something more, something I hardly dared admit even to myself. I could have faced a man, maybe, even a man with a gun or other weapon. But the thought of seeing that transformation again made me sick with a bone-deep sickness, a sort of paralysis. People throw around the word *horror* pretty easily these days, but I had a feeling I'd just had a taste of the real thing.

Just the same, it went against me to sit there and wait without doing anything to help ourselves. I felt that if I knew more about the *dikri*, it might help a little. No matter how repulsive and horrible they were, it made no sense to react so emotionally. I said, 'I gather everybody hates the *dikri*, but why? Is it only because they are against you? Or because everyone is afraid of that werewolf, or weredragon act they do?'

Karsten said, 'No, there are other shape-changing races, some of them less human in appearance than the *dikri*, but they are – well, this sounds like a paradox – more *human*. The *dikri* are cold and ruthless – unemotional. We call a brutal sadist inhuman because he has none of that fellow-feeling which men feel for their own kind. And most intelligent races, human or nonhuman, have some sense of kinship among all living creatures. They'll kill other living things which threaten them, or if they want to eat them, but not wantonly. The *dikri*, though, are like your sharks; they have no sense of kinship even with their own kind. If a *dikri* is wounded, his fellow-*dikri* will kill or attack him at once simply because he impairs the perfection of their kind. There is no way we can communicate with them; they will not obey laws or keep treaties, and the worst of it is, they also are an intelligent race. If they were merely vicious animals we could exterminate them for the good of Cosmos.'

'It sounds like a hopeless proposition,' I said, 'but I have a feeling if I were in your people's shoes I'd forget about their intelligence and exterminate them anyway.'

Karsten looked disgusted. 'And then,' he commented, 'We should be no better than they, and have no more right to survive. Less, really, since we know better and they apparently do not.'

I gave up. Our minds just weren't meeting, but I had the uncomfortable feeling that I sounded like the backwoods barbarian to a Galactic citizen.

Karsten's aesthetic sensitivities about killing off the poor benighted *dikri* might be very civilized, but if his race had survived this long, they must have some common sense about survival. I said, 'Well, I hope your scruples don't prevent you from killing this particular specimen if we get a chance.'

'Rellin?' His face twisted. 'I would kill him with my bare hands if I had the strength!'

I looked at Karsten's bleeding arm and white face, and said, 'Obviously, you haven't. But there ought to be some way we can even up the odds. I don't know if we can tackle the dragon–' I touched the claw-wound on my face. 'But if he comes in here looking human, maybe we can do something. If these seats weren't fastened down, maybe we could whack him over the head with one of them.'

Karsten looked at me with something like admiration. 'I would never have thought of that. They unbolt at the base, of course.' I was already kneeling to unbolt one of them; finding that the bolts would not turn with my fingers, I swore softly, but Karsten was kneeling by Harret's body. He fished from the dead man's pockets a small tool kit and tossed it to me; there was an ingenious arrangement of detachable wrench and screwdriver heads which fitted into a small porcelain handle, and the maddest thing about it was that the handle was decorated with small flower designs in electric blue and fluorescent pink. In our culture it would have been a special Little Old Lady toolkit, and yet the damned thing was brutally efficient. There was even a four-inch knife blade, and after I had the seat unbolted I screwed the knife blade into the handle and said, 'I'll hang on to this.'

'A – a blade? Against his weapons?'

'A knife not much bigger than this made a bloody mess, and I do mean bloody, of your shoulder,' I pointed out. 'I don't know if those *dikri* chaps have blood or not, but whatever they have in place of it, I'm going to try to find out.'

He said, 'Not being a technician, I have no such tool kit, but—' He went to the control panel, and took up a hefty wrench-like thing and deliberately smashed the glass; he broke off a sharp splinter. 'This might be of some use.'

I had my doubts, but I nodded approval. Then we sat down to wait, one on either side of the door opening.

It seemed like a long time, though I don't suppose

it was more than three-quarters of an hour or so, before the lock handle began slowly to turn.

'Take it easy,' I warned in a whisper. 'They might shove your father through first. We don't want to brain *him*.'

The warning was just in time; the door widened and Varzil stumbled through. He looked doped, glassy-eyed, but at least he was alive. Behind him one of the slab-faced humanoids moved, weapon at the ready; it stepped through, its eyes and weapon fast on Varzil – and I leaped and brought the heavy metal seat crashing down.

The *dikri* dropped like a stone, twisting and writhing; I leaped on top of it, Karsten beside me. I brought the knife blade down and shoved it into its throat. It went in so easily I felt a little sick. Then, just as I relaxed, there was a twisting, convulsive spasm; steely muscles threw me off and backwards, and Karsten went reeling. I struck my head against the metal seat I had used to brain the *dikri* with, and lay there half-stunned, every minute expecting a flash of searing heat that would broil me to death.

None came. Karsten picked himself up and said in a dazed voice, 'It's dead!'

'It's still moving!'

Varzil said, a trifle thickly, 'Their muscles go into spasm after death; it will continue to twitch like that for hours. But oh, yes, it is dead.'

I looked down at the still horribly-twitching dragon-form into which the dying *dikri* had metamorphosed with its dying convulsion. I wanted to throw up, and at the same time I wanted to cry, and together with both of these I felt a momentary exultation. I'd killed the damned thing! I'd never killed so much as a mouse before and theoretically at least I was a pacifist, but I figured most pacifists had never been in a corner like this. I stood trying to get back my breath and decide what to do next; then I realized that the open door through which Varzil and the *dikri* had come had suddenly swung shut and the lock snapped.

We had killed a *dikri* – but we were still locked in, and our ship was still fast to the *dikri* ship; we weren't a damned bit better off than we were before.

At least Varzil was back alive. I hadn't realized, until I saw him walk in safe and sound, how much I really had liked the old man. He was shaking his head.

'You might both have been killed,' he said reprovingly. 'And you have helped nothing.'

Karsten was holding his father's hand tightly. 'But – did they hurt you, Father?'

'Nothing so crude,' Varzil said with a little smile. 'Even the *dikri* need not resort to physical torture, and when they found out with their little brain-probes that I had not the information they wished for, they let me go again. I was sure that would happen.' He put his hands to his head. 'I have nothing worse than a bad headache from their methods of questioning.'

'Which means,' Karsten said, putting into words the thought that crossed my mind, 'that now none of us are of any use to them – and they may very well come and finish us off as they did Harret.'

Varzil looked grave. 'I think, if they planned that, they would never have brought me back into the saucer. Nothing would have been easier for them than to cut me down when they finished questioning, or simply to cut our saucer adrift, first dismantling the drives, so that we died in space. I think they plan something else for us – but I do not know what.'

He was silent, taking up a blanket from a compartment under one of the seats and throwing it over the dead *dikri*. I was glad to have the still-twitching corpse out of sight. When I was a kid I'd heard that if you killed a snake it would keep twitching till sundown. I'd never believed it. I did now.

Then we all sat around and waited.

We didn't talk; we all had plenty to think about. I tried not to think about home, about Nina and Father and Win. It was pretty obvious I wouldn't be released, as Varzil had promised, in several hours. Nor did I stop to think that I was actually out in space, where nobody on Earth except a few of the astronauts in space capsules had ever gone before. That didn't bear thinking about, or I'd have been scared out of my wits. I tried hard not to think about the corpses on the floor, either. Mostly I just sat and waited to see what would happen next. There was nothing else to do, and at least we weren't dead yet. It's funny; you think of an adventure as being exciting, or terrifying, or interesting, but never of being just plain boring. Yet that is exactly what this part was; we sat, waiting, and it was as boring as waiting for the dentist to get started.

Varzil got up once and inspected the panel we had smashed. He said, 'I wanted to make sure you hadn't damaged the communicator. There is a bare possibility they might cut us adrift somewhere they believe we can't be rescued from, and if the communicator can function we might have a chance."

'No,' Karsten said. 'I smashed that particular

panel on purpose. I knew we wouldn't need the stellar-field reader, whatever happened.'

Varzil said to me, 'I am sorry you became involved in this. Don't give up hope yet; there are very severe laws against interfering with the inhabitants of a neutral planet.'

'When did laws ever stop Rellin and his kind?' Karsten demanded bitterly.

'Yet, they may prefer not to break them too openly. Just as they knew that if I disappeared without trace, the Commissioners' Council would never abandon the search. Be assured, whatever they do to us, they will try to make it look like a natural disappearance; and we may have a chance. I should be deceiving you if I told you it would be any more than a very slim chance; but it might be a chance for life. If we keep our wits about us, we may live through this. So don't despair yet.'

I wasn't despairing. I guess nobody ever believes definitely that they're going to die; at least as long as they are physically intact and unwounded, with food and air to breathe and, for the moment, safety. I was scared, but there's something inside that keeps you believing, right to the last moment, that everything's going to be all right, the Marines will land or something.

Varzil motioned to us both to take stock of our remaining supplies. 'It's obvious they aren't going to kill us out of hand, or crash our saucer into the moon to make it look as if we'd landed there.'

I asked, 'What *are* the possibilities? What *could* they do with us?'

'I doubt if they'll simply cut us adrift in space now. If we were ever found – this saucer could be traced by the detection-beams – it would be easy to guess that we wouldn't simply have missed our rendezvous with the mother-ship.'

I asked, 'Won't your ship start looking for you when you are overdue for the rendezvous?'

'Not a chance,' he said rather soberly. 'The cost and difficulty of manoeuvring one of the interstellar ships inside the field of a sun is prohibitive. They are kept in parking orbits fairly far out. Of course, they have rescue ships on board, and if we could get out a distress call they could send a saucer for us. But our communicator will not operate within the field generated by the *dikri* ship. No, I think they will keep us fast to them until we are well past the orbit of the mother ship, the ship of the Commission. After that – well, it is anyone's guess.'

Later, to while away the time – and there was plenty of it hanging on our hands by now – I asked Varzil something about his people, and what they were doing on Earth. He had been evasive about my questions before; now he didn't hesitate to answer, and that gave me my own ideas about our chances of coming through alive.

His people, who lived on a planet of Spica which had a name that sounded like *Branntol*, were one part of a confederation of planetary governments that took in fifteen or twenty star systems and about seventy planets. They were making a scientific survey of all inhabited planets in their area, to determine which ones could be taken into the Federation and which ones should be left alone to develop further and avoid cultural shock.

Planets like Earth were taboo, but there were a few outlaws – among whom, I gathered, the *dikri* were numbered – who liked unsurveyed planets, and couldn't be kept out of them. Sometimes they exploited the natives ruthlessly for their natural resources. Sometimes they merely used the planets as playgrounds for their private games, which, I gathered, were war games and left the planet in question quite a mess. The Confederation did the best it could to keep them away from unprotected planets, but there were something like forty thousand unsurveyed planets already listed, and about as many more they hadn't got to yet; the whole project was contemplated in terms of millennia, not decades or even centuries, and meanwhile, the Confederation couldn't possibly keep a cop on every planet just to scare away the *dikri* and their kind.

Normally the *dikri* simply tried to operate in areas where the Confederation hadn't set up yet, because if provoked the Confederation *would* exercise some sort of sanctions against the *dikri*. Varzil didn't tell me what they were and I didn't ask, but I imagined they were fairly drastic, because the *dikri* were willing to go to some lengths to avoid them.

In fact, I gathered that was the one hope we had – that an individual *dikri*, or group, like Rellin, would not risk bringing Federation machinery into action. 'Even the *dikri*,' said Varzil, 'do not like to – what is your phrase? – don't like to play with fire.'

We had eaten again, and slept, and repeated both of these two or three times, when a slow whicking sound began within the cabin, and the slow range of rainbow lights began to move within the saucer. I jerked erect out of a brief doze, and sat up, blinking, and wondered what would happen next.

'The *dikri* ship is decelerating,' Varzil said. 'The

lights are a speed-range device, and operate automatically in here.'

'Where are we, Father?' Karsten asked.

Varzil went to the instruments and said, 'The space instruments, of course, are not working. But if we are coming inside a planet's gravitational field, I may be able to get a reading from the magnetic ones.'

'Could they have taken us back to Earth?'

Varzil hesitated, unwilling to damp the hope in his son's face, then said honestly, 'I think it unlikely. We were only nine hours off Earth, at saucer speeds, when we were intercepted; to take us back would have required little more than that. The *dikri* ships manoeuvre, within a solar system, a little more easily than our interstellar carriers but not nearly as well as our saucers. We are most likely somewhere near the orbit of Mars.'

I stored that away in my mind. We had been in space now about four days, I supposed. Everyone knew the figure of five days in free-fall, between the Earth and the Moon, so evidently they weren't bound by Earth's limiting speeds. Very likely their interstellar ships went faster than light, since Karsten was young enough not to have spent light years in space.

The lights continued flickering inside the cabin; blue, crimson, amber, green. I felt a curious, sick, empty feeling in my head and stomach which I supposed was the process of deceleration. Varzil and Karsten fastened their seat straps and bars and ordered me to do the same. The two dead bodies on the floor began to slide around and the blankets came off them, and maybe the less said about that, the better.

Then we hit with a bump and a bang and the saucer's lights flicked off and everything was quiet; it didn't help a bit to know I was probably the first Earthman to land on Mars.

CHAPTER NINE

As soon as we were safely down, Varzil was tearing at his safety straps. 'Barry, get that seat again!' He was kneeling by the dead *dikri*, and when he straightened he had the creature's weapon in his hand. Karsten tried to unfasten his belt but could not manage it; I realized that without medical attention he would be in very serious trouble. I hoisted the seat over my head, flattening myself out next to the door of the saucer, as the lock began to turn.

A gap widened, and the familiar thick head of a *dikri* in human form thrust itself through; I brought the seat crashing down, struck it a glancing blow, and was thrown in the reflex of the thing's metamorphosis halfway across the cabin. There was a flare of blue fire from Varzil's weapon, an inhuman howl of rage; then the saucer was crowded with three, four, five of the monsters and I knew we were licked. Nothing human could have bested four of the things in hand-to-hand combat.

I dragged myself to a sitting position on the floor and looked up bitterly, hating, at the slab-faced form of Rellin, at the others, wondering how anyone could ever mistake them for men.

Rellin said, in his thick voice: 'I see you killed Carandal. I thought that had happened.' It pushed the dead *dikri* slightly with its foot; glanced sideways at the writhing one I had bashed with the seat, lowered its weapon and shot it. Karsten had prepared me for this kind of callousness, but nevertheless I turned sick as I watched. Varzil was struggling between two other *dikri*; Rellin came and took the weapon from his hand, then said indifferently, 'Let him go.'

They released Varzil, who stood breathing hard, looking sick and exhausted. Rellin said, 'We are not going to kill you.'

I withheld any shouts of whoopee. I was fairly sure there was a catch to this. Varzil said, hoarsely, fighting for breath, 'Rellin, I warn you. The boy' – he pointed to me – 'is a neutral, a native. Harm him and the Confederation will never let up on you.'

'I told you we do not mean to harm you,' Rellin said, and smiled. Or, rather, its mouth stretched in a terrible parody of a smile. 'It is none of my doing if your craft attached itself to mine in space.

'Let them out.' Rellin gestured roughly.

The door gaped, and as one of the *dikri* advanced on me, I moved towards it. I felt my heart catch and turn over. A blast of icy wind raked at me. Then a rough paw thrust me through it; I groped for the steps with my feet, stumbled, fell full-length and lay sprawled, gasping in the bitter cold, on the surface of Mars. Behind me, Varzil stumbled down the steps, holding Karsten carefully with one arm. The *dikri* hoisted the dead bodies out; dropped them beside us. I stood watching, in dumb horror, as the saucer door closed and lights began to blink on and off at the edges.

I looked up then and saw the *dikri* ship, huge and strange, glowing with the cold phosphorescence of a great sea slug, our saucer like a big glowing blister at its side. There was a soft whickering, whirring noise.

Then the two ships rose together, still joined; slowly gained speed, then rose further and further, grew smaller and smaller till they were only a pinpoint in the thin purple sky, and were gone.

We were alone, marooned on Mars. At our feet lay the dead bodies of Harret and the *dikri*. There was nothing else in sight.

Nothing.

Nothing at all.

In short, we were dead.

I don't remember very well what happened in the next few minutes. I think I may have gone a little crazy. I remember hearing Varzil cursing in a steady stream, in the language I didn't know, but anyone could have known that he was cursing the *dikri* in every foul term he knew. Karsten just stood there looking faint and dazed, and finally dropped to his hands and knees and crouched, shivering – and I think that brought us to our senses.

For the first time I began to realize what had happened, to take it in. The first thing I realized was that I was breathing. I'm no expert, but I'd kept up with the reports of the satellites, and I'd understood there wasn't enough air on Mars to support a cat, let alone a human. Just the same, I was breathing. It wasn't easy, the wind was blowing a gale and took the breath right out of my nostrils, but just the same I was breathing. So much for the experts.

And *cold*! I imagined it must be like this at the South Pole; only of course there was no snow. All around us, a dull grey-brown sand, littered with low green and blue rocks, lay undulating faintly in the wind. A few thick spiky plants, like a Salvador Dali version of cactus, broke the landscape at odd points.

Apart from that, as far as the eye could see, there was nothing; at an immeasurably far point, the grey-brown sand merged into dull blue and purple and blended imperceptibly with the sky. About forty degrees above the invisible horizon point, a tiny glowing red ball, the size of a thumbail, hung in the sky to show where the sun theoretically was. I shivered in my heavy coat and wished I had four of them on top of each other. It was going to be bad enough starving to death in this howling desert – without freezing to death first!

I turned my head finally towards Varzil, who stood with his hands absently on Karsten's shoulder. He was watching me, and I felt like cursing him, and the impulse that had led me to help Karsten, and had brought me to die here. I thought, suddenly and crazily, of Nina putting supper on the table and asking herself aloud, the way I'd heard her once, as I came in the back door unexpectedly: 'Where on earth *is* that boy?' A lump clogged my throat. My mother and father would never know whether I was alive or dead, or that I was nowhere on Earth at all. I opened my mouth to yell that it was all his fault and I'd never wanted to get mixed up in his damned Galactic politics, then shut it again. He and Karsten were going to die too and I didn't suppose they were any too crazy about the idea. So I asked instead, 'Is Karsten okay?'

'He is very far from well,' Varzil said gravely. 'If we cannot get him out of this cold, and find medical help for him soon, he will never be better.'

I said, rather grimly, 'You don't happen to know of a good hotel around here, do you?'

Karsten laughed, a weak, improbable sound. He

said, in a ghost's voice, 'And to think I was furious that we had to be saddled with a native, a planetary, who would give up if things looked bad! I feel better already.'

'As for giving up when things look bad,' I said, with my mouth tight, 'my great-grandfather came over the Rockies and wintered in the Donner Pass with the Patrick Breen party, which wasn't exactly a picnic. I'll back a California pioneer against one of your people any old day!'

Varzil said, 'If you take it in that spirit it may not be as bad as we fear; yet I must warn you, our condition is desperate.' He moved a little to the lee of the dead bodies, lowered Karsten to the sand, and said, 'Help me to pile these up to make a shelter.'

My face must have showed my horror, for he said sharply, 'I beg of you! We have no time for sentiment or squeamishness! They will guard us a little against the wind, and one of the *dikri* has still a little body warmth.'

It was still twitching, too, and it wasn't the most pleasant thing I'd ever done; but when Varzil instructed me to strip the dead man and the dead *dikri*, I protested, in a rage, 'I'm no corpse-robber!'

'You may die with your scruples, then,' Varzil said. 'Warm clothing is warm clothing, and it is no good to Harret, may he rest in peace. Also, Harret has a few small tools in his pocket; and there is no telling what the *dikri* may have in their clothing.'

I apologized and obeyed. Just the same, I told myself as I hauled gingerly at the twitching corpse, if Varzil carried good sense one step farther I probably would mutiny. I'd rather starve than try to make a meal of *dikri* steak or hamburger.

I turned the assortment of oddments from Harret's pocket over to Karsten, then tackled the corpses of the dead *dikri*. They each had a small round transparent thing something like a compass, assorted papers and printed cards apiece; one was carrying a packet of Kleenex, which give me a sort of cold shiver, wondering where he had bought it and thinking about the unsuspecting human who had sold it to him. And each had a small brass token in which I recognized a conventional dragon-shape, or *dikri*-shape. Varzil examined all these things, turning the dragon-shape between his hands.

Karsten weakly asked what they were, and Varzil said, 'Keys. Starting keys for the smaller individual ships of the *dikri*; like our saucers but less convenient. Which is why they wanted our saucer, of course.'

I couldn't help it. The idea of a flying saucer starting with an ignition key like any old Ford or Chevy was too much for me. I said, laughing almost hysterically, 'Don't help a good boy go bad. Lock your car. Take your keys!' Karsten chimed in, 'Now, if we can just find one of those things parked in the next lot . . .'

Varzil said, 'You never can tell,' put the two brass things in his pocket, and bent over Karsten, putting a thing very much like a flashlight in my hand. 'I must see to that knife-wound. Help me, now, and be quiet.'

When Karsten was bandaged, and the extra clothing from the dead shared out – it came in handy, I had to admit, including the thick heavy cloak of a *dikri* which fell to my share – we huddled in the lee of the corpses, trying to share body warmth and shelter against the biting wind.

'We cannot stay here,' Varzil said, not telling me

anything I didn't know. The corpses were already beginning to freeze, and I knew damned well that if we stayed still we'd be in the same shape in a few hours. Karsten didn't speak – he seemed to be in shock – so I played straight man. 'We can't stay here and we can't go anywhere else – or am I missing something in the landscape? Don't tell me the *dikri* considerately dropped us off in easy walking distance from a luxury underground hotel for distressed spacemen?'

'No,' Varzil said. 'Unfortunately. I am not even certain where we are. But this planet is used – now and again – for coming and going, both by the Confederation and by the *dikri*. I do not think they would land us in Confederation territory, but I read our field instruments before the saucer landed. We are near the twelfth parallel, and see–' He pointed, and very dimly, through the haze and the gathering darkness, I made out a low line of grey hills. 'There are caves there, and I have heard that the *dikri* have built shelters there. We might find one unoccupied. It is our only chance; we must have shelter before a sand-blizzard comes. They are not infrequent in this season – and the season is just beginning.'

I wasn't crazy about the idea of finding shelter in any place frequented by *dikri*, but I supposed he'd thought of that, so I didn't say anything. Anyway, we'd never get there. I only asked, 'Can Karsten walk?'

'It is better to die on the way to shelter than to die doing nothing,' Varzil said stolidly. 'But for now we will rest; then we will go.'

While the sun dipped towards the invisible horizon and sank, we crouched beneath the bodies of the man and the dead *dikri*, and shivered, and waited. That night was grim. I'm no more imaginative than most people, but we had three corpses for company, and the *dikri* corpse closest to me was still twitching; every now and then a sharp spasm would run through it and every time it happened I'd go into a spasm too. I was glad when it froze, even though it was colder that way, like huddling up against solid ice.

I didn't know, then, how long the Martian night was, but by the time that little pink glob of sun was above the horizon, I was ready to say it was too long. I was cramped and cold in every limb. Although the barricade of frozen bodies had been some shelter, the wind cut like a knife and my face felt half frozen. I hadn't slept for a moment. Nevertheless, when Varzil stretched and stood up, beating his hands together to try to warm them, I was ready to start off. Anything was better than this.

Karsten, though stiff and evidently sore, looked better than the night before. The only explanation I can give is that rest – such as it was, though I personally didn't feel rested – had helped, or that the intense cold had semi-anaesthetized and numbed his arm. His voice seemed stronger, and when Varzil took from his pockets a packet of the rations, divided it in equal pieces and passed them around, he ate hungrily. So, for that matter, did I. It seemed an awfully long time since I'd had a square meal.

Then Varzil took a compass from his pocket, studied it intently for a long time, squinted up at the sun through it, finally pointed and said, 'This way. Let's go.' And we went.

We just started walking. And kept on. And on. And on.

The next period of time is one of the worst in my memory. We walked. The wind cut, and gritty sand kept whirling up and blowing. During one of our infrequent halts to rest – we would walk about two hours and rest about ten minutes – I scooped up a little of the sand and looked at it closely. It looked like fine emery powder, or ground iron filings, and felt like it when it blew against you or got in your eyes. After a while my skin was raw; we all took off some dispensable undergarment and wound it around our faces, up to the eyes, and if it was thin enough, over them. You can see through cotton undershirt material, I found out, if you put only one thickness over your eyes. You can't see very *well*, but then, on Mars there's no scenery and you don't miss much anyhow.

The air was so cold that with every breath I felt as if I were drawing down solid ice into my lungs, and this made thirst rasp my throat until I was gasping with it. But there was nothing I could do about it. Before long I was plodding along over the lumpy, trackless sand in a daze, dreaming about huge cups of hot coffee, refrigerators crammed with cartons of milk, taps flowing streams of steaming hot water to bathe in, icy water to gulp down my parched throat. It was slow, monotonous slogging underfoot; stones and sand, sand and stones, with some thick hairy softer stuff intermittently easing the walking – it felt a little like moss.

It got to where I hated to breathe because of the way it made my throat drier and drier. When we paused about the fourth time for a rest and a bite of the dried ration, I couldn't chew it at all, hungry as I was.

'Try to eat,' Varzil said. 'The food will transform itself into heat.' He kept doggedly chewing at his own ration, but his mouth, too, looked blue and parched. Karsten had said his father was 'not strong' but so far he was the toughest of us all.

The sun got higher until, at what must have been high noon, it was about as bright as it might have been on a foggy day in London; then it began to slide down again and get duller and darker still. And we kept moving, but the line of hills for which we were heading didn't seem to get any closer.

A while before sundown we ate the last scrap of food; and as the night closed in we stretched out, huddled close together in the lee of some low rocks, for the interminable hours of darkness. I lay on the inside, with Karsten next to me, and Varzil at the outside, and we piled all the *dikri* garments like blankets over the top. Varzil, evidently exhausted, slept with soft gasping snores.

Despite my exhaustion, I couldn't sleep. I was parched and famished, with cramps in my stomach, and a sore throat which could hardly gather enough moisture to swallow. During a lot of that night I think I was having hallucinations. I thought I was at home, with Win setting the supper table and the smell of pizza wafting deliciously through the air. But just as I'd start to take a bite I'd come to myself again and be under those damned rocks on Mars, with Varzil snoring and Karsten moaning softly in his sleep. I wondered how they could sleep, and if this would be our last night of life; if Varzil thought that without food, water and fire we could reach any place at all before we died.

I did sleep a little at last, nightmarishly, but as

morning thinned the darkness a little, I was so cold and parched that when Varzil stood up, stiffly stretching his cramped limbs, I didn't move. What was the point of another day like the last? Why not die here where we could do it a little more easily? Why keep putting one damned exhausted foot in front of the other until we fell in our tracks? Karsten hauled at me, but I shoved him away and covered my head with my arms.

'Go 'way,' I mumbled. 'Not goin' any further. No place to go anyway. Goin' stay right here.'

'What is there to stay here for?' I heard Karsten say, but I was too far gone for logic and persuasion. If I could only sleep . . .

Varzil said, 'We can't carry him,' and Karsten said, 'I won't leave him. If he hadn't saved my life he would have been safe at home.'

I felt Varzil grab my shoulder and drag at me again. He said, in a voice which seemed like the tolling of a bell, 'We brought you here; we won't abandon you. If you will not get up and help to save us all, we will have to stay and die with you. Is that what you want?'

Of all the damnably unfair ways to put it, I thought foggily through the great haze of sleep. Did they want me to be responsible for killing them? I grumbled, 'Oh, if you put it that way,' and hauled myself woozily upright.

Varzil's eyes were inflamed and sunken in his sand-rimed face. Karsten looked thinner, paler, his eyes bright with fever, and he tried not to move his bad arm at all. I didn't even want to think about what I must have looked like. My throat was such torture I could neither swallow nor speak. I sank into sick apathy, lifting one foot drearily after the other and putting it down with a thump that seemed to jolt my whole sore body.

The day dragged on interminably. During one of the breathing spells – we had stopped talking now – I found myself looking around with a perilous, dying clarity.

We would die. Was there nothing to be done? There was no fire, and no way to make it. You couldn't rub two sticks where there was no plant life and no wood. In a desert on Earth, even the worst, there were animals to trap and plants edible and otherwise, if you knew the difference. Men trained in survival techniques had lived even in the Arctic and Death Valley. But here? There didn't seem to be an animal alive anywhere, and the moss underfoot didn't look promising, nor the nightmarish stuff that looked like cactus–

Cactus.

If it was cactus, how did it grow? Nothing living grew without water; I knew that much. I suddenly remembered what every Californian child knows. I dug in my pockets, finding my student card from Berkeley High and a couple of ball point pens. I tossed the card away, thinking insane thoughts about litter bugs, and then my hand closed around the knife I had used on the *dikri*. Shuddering, I tried to ignore the weird stains towards the tip, and tested the edge on my finger. Varzil, slumped with his eyes shut, suddenly opened his eyes and rushed at me, trying to wrest the knife away.

I exploded in rage: 'Did you think I was going to kill and eat you? Damn it, leave me alone a minute; I want to try something!'

Varzil said, hoarsely but with dignity, 'It was your own death wish I feared.'

I paid no attention. Now that I had this idea nothing was further from my mind than dying, but I hadn't the breath to waste. I headed towards one of the cactus-like growths.

The stuff was anywhere from eight inches to two feet in height, a dirty-looking no-colour with reddish-veined bulgy protuberances. I got down on my knees, almost holding my breath. I dug my knife into one of the bulges.

The plant screamed at me!

I know in retrospect that it was only escaping air; but it flung me back on my heels and I almost drove the knife into my palm out of sheer shock. It was a high, eldritch whine, with a weirdly human sound. Then I smelled a clear, tangy smell and I knew that death had suddenly turned to life, for a thin, clear, watery fluid was oozing from the cactus.

I sawed at the plant again with my knife and brought the dripping stem to my lips. It occurred to me at the last moment that it might be poison, but at that moment, parched as I was, I didn't even care about that. It was *wet*.

My lips soaked up the precious fluid. For a minute I couldn't even have told you what it tasted like; then I realized it had a sweetish, vaguely acid taste. It was icy cold, of course, cold enough to hurt my teeth, but who cared about that?

After a minute, when I had sucked enough to appease that first awful dryness, I remembered my companions. I sawed off a gourd-like leaf for Karsten, handed it to him, then gave Varzil the knife to cut himself a chunk while I went back to sucking and chewing on the delicious moisture.

For the next half hour we didn't do anything else. We hacked off bulby leaves of the Martian cactus and sucked and chewed them to pulp, extracting the last drops of moisture. The fibres were woody rather than succulent, and the taste was vaguely like broccoli with sawdust, but in our condition it tasted just fine.

And there was plenty of it. There was a whole planetful of it, and no Martian to come and bawl us out for robbing his watermelon patch.

At last, unbelievably, we had had enough. It was about then that I realized how cold I still was, and that the icy, gritty wind seemed stronger than ever, knifing at my face and hands until they were half frozen. There's no way to describe the terrible, slamming violence of that wind, and the silence of it. People think of wind as noisy. That's because what they hear is wind in the trees or beating around buildings and corners. This wind didn't beat around anything. It just swept for hundreds of miles over nothing but sand. I thrust my hands in under my coat and stood there, shivering, no longer thirsty, but hungry and freezing.

Varzil said at last, 'This should help us. The hills are further than I thought. That was a good idea of yours, Barry. It had never occurred to me that this vegetation was edible.'

I said, 'About those hills of yours. Will we be any better off when we reach them? Or will it just be another place we can starve and freeze in?'

'I know there are shelters there,' Varzil said, 'but I cannot be sure we will find them. Or what they will have for our comfort. This is a chance – no more than a chance.' He looked at Karsten and his lips pressed tight together. I knew what he was thinking; could the kid make it?

It wasn't quite so bad walking now, without the torture of thirst; but my muscles ached with the cold and I felt that my hands and especially my feet were beginning to freeze. My shoes had never been meant for long hiking, and my socks were a caked mess of sweat, dirt and ice. Every time I set foot down I felt a new blister forming. We slogged and slogged, and I felt as if I had been walking forever, cold, frozen, in pain. I drew up the improvised sand-mask over my eyes and walked in a dark dream, not knowing or caring where I went. Vaguely I knew, when we stopped to rest a few minutes and gulp down a little more of the acrid cactus-juice, that the wind was dropping; but I was unprepared for Karsten's cry:

'Look – look there!'

Through the clearing sand as the wind dropped, the hills were clearly visible: low ramparts of blue rock, stained with rusty darkness, worn away by endless erosion into sand. They were no more than five miles distant. But five miles in our present condition – and then how far to find shelter?

Varzil was scanning them, sheltering his eyes against the sand with his cupped hands. I saw how red-rimmed and inflamed his eyes were, and knew my own were just as bad. Finally Varzil pointed.

'An irregularity in the line there,' he said. 'It might be some sort of building.'

I couldn't see it. Neither could Karsten, though he looked for a long time. Nevertheless, by silent consent, we all headed for it. The chance was better than nothing.

We were all stumbling now, half-blind, exhausted, three spectres in the endless desert. Each step I took seemed to get me nowhere, and I walked in an apathetic daze, without hope, not even caring much any more. When we got there, what would we find? A cold shelter of bare boards, empty, fireless, foodless? Or the warm and tender hospitality of the *dikri*? At least they seemed to have no interest in tormenting human beings; they'd shoot us down with no more compunction than I'd kill a fly.

During the last awful few miles I gave myself up almost completely to self-pity. I dragged along, not caring what happened to me or to my companions. Until Karsten cried out, stumbled and fell headlong in the sand.

I knew this was the end. We would never reach the shelter, if there was any shelter.

Varzil knelt beside his son and I heard him talking in their own language, coaxing, pleading, threatening, I didn't listen. I was having hallucinations again. In the bare sand, with my head between my knees for less resistance to the terrible wind, I was once again smelling the spicy, wonderful smell of pizza. It's funny what hunger does to you . . . hunger and a diet of broccoli-flavoured cactus-juice. It tantalized me to the point of sickness. Karsten lay in the sand, not moving, and I wished it were me. He wasn't worrying. I wondered if he were dead.

I dragged myself up and shielded my face against the blowing sand again. I said to Varzil, 'is he all right?'

Varzil shook his head. 'He has been at the edge of collapse for more than a day now. His strength is finished.'

I said doggedly, 'I guess we can carry him. If it isn't too far.'

I knew it would be too far, as soon as we hoisted him between us. Five hundred feet would be too far, in the condition we were in. Holding Karsten between us, we could no longer shield our faces from the wind with our arms. My face was numb, and I realized my cheeks were frozen. I couldn't feel my feet any more, and that was just as well.

The wind was dropping. Maybe we were under the lee of the hills now. I couldn't raise my eyes to see, but Varzil said shakily, between gasps for breath, 'I think – I see – a building.'

I don't even remember when the wind died. I only know that I heard Varzil cry out with triumph. I stumbled forward into warmth and light, fell on top of Karsten; he moved and I was surprised to realize he wasn't dead. And that was the last thing I knew for a long, long time. I fell asleep right there where I had fallen.

CHAPTER TEN

When I woke up, I was lying on a floor of some smooth stuff, but my head was on a pillow and my shoes had been hauled off, and my feet were warm.

We were inside a little, dimly-lit, circular building. Karsten lay in a low bed, covered with the *dikri* cloak, Varzil slumbered on the floor at his side. I hauled myself upright, looking down at my feet. They were warm and, although dirty and blackened in spots, none of the toes seemed seriously damaged.

Varzil opened his eyes and looked at me.

I said, 'How's Karsten? And what's for dinner? In that order. And after that, where are we?'

'We are in one of the *dikri* shelters,' Varzil said. 'It is deserted and possibly forgotten, so there is no need to be worried about them. Karsten is better; I have looked at his shoulder and it is healing. As for food, I don't know. We must look around.'

We started hunting in the various cupboards and built-in storage spots right then. We found a few empty packages and a half dozen full ones. The stuff inside could have been soap or silver polish for all I knew, but Varzil said it was a special emergency ration, made unpalatable on purpose so that people would eat the bare minimum for survival; I supposed it was better than nothing.

Varzil still seemed troubled, and I asked if Karsten was really so bad.

'No,' he said, 'but the wind has died down.'

'Wonderful,' I said, 'beautiful. We can get along fine without it.'

'You don't understand. This means we are in the eye of a sand-hurricane. Winter is closing in – and in winter there are sand-blizzards in which nothing can live. If the winter season closes in before we can get away from here–'

He didn't finish, and I knew he had been planning some form of rescue.

There were two doors to the building: the one we'd come in by, now closed tightly against the outdoors, and another. Varzil pushed against it; it was locked and handleless, with only a round hole in the centre, like a keyhole. He hesitated a moment, then took out of his pocket the small brass dragon-shaped thing he had removed from the body of the *dikri*. It slid easily into the hole; he twisted and the door opened.

Stairs led downwards; slowly and cautiously, we went down.

The stairs ended and we came out into a sunken room. It was large – and damp. *Damp!* on dry, waterless Mars? But unmistakably, water was trickling from the stone walls; this was evidently an underground cave, and with some source of water. I breathed more freely. The room was so dark and shadowy that at first I did not notice the great, humped mound in the centre, until Varzil laid his hand on my arm, and pointed.

It was a flying saucer.

It wasn't Varzil's. It was larger, painted a drab grey, with curious striations which I supposed were some alien form of identification markings. It was clumsier, too. But it was a saucer – and we had the keys! We could get away from here! We were safe; we were saved! I saw myself back on Earth in a few more days, with only the memory of a great adventure. I let out a whoop.

'Don't rejoice too soon,' Varzil said. 'This means the place is not forgotten – the *dikri* owners may return to claim their property.'

'Then the thing to do is get out of here in a hurry!' I retorted. I was ready to climb on board right then. Varzil rebuked, 'It is not so simple. The wind is rising again, and a Martian sand-blizzard can blow an interstellar ship out of the sky, let alone a small craft like this. We are all still exhausted. And worst of all – I do not know how to operate the *dikri* craft. I suppose one saucer is much like another, but I can never be sure. I will have to study the craft, perhaps for days, before I can safely take it up even for a short flight. Calm yourself and let us go back.'

I might have been sore at what Varzil said, only it made too much sense. As we turned back I noticed a pizza smell. Was I hallucinating again? 'What is that marvellous smell?'

Varzil looked around briefly. Then he hurried to the side of the shed, and there, in a soaking tank full of water, the smell emerged fuller and spicier than ever; something that looked like moss was half submerged in reddish-looking water, and smelled exactly like hot pizza baking. It smelled so delicious I could have devoured it as it was.

'Martian lichens,' Varzil said. 'I did not think of them on the desert because they are poisonous in the raw state; but when soaked and boiled, they are edible and even palatable. It seems that we will not starve, however long we stay here.'

'Just the same, I hope it won't be long,' I retorted as I followed him up the stairs.

Except for the ever-present worry about one of the *dikri* coming back, the next few days would have been a picnic after the last. We had plenty to eat and enough to drink. Karsten slowly recovered his strength, and the lichen, boiled up like beans, had the spicy smell and taste which made me think of spaghetti. The *dikri* shelter was no palace, but it was better than the desert by a long shot, and it was easier to breathe. Artificial oxygen was released by feeding sand into oxidating machinery, and the sand, being various copper and iron oxides, released its oxygen with due process.

Every day Varzil went down to crawl inside the *dikri* saucer and study the controls, and finally announced that if we ever got a lull in the windstorm – which now seemed perpetual – he thought he could fly it. Not between planets, but there was a small Federation base near one of the polar domes, and he thought he could get it that far.

I asked if there was a radio or some form of communicator on board through which he could send a message, and got the discouraging but unsurprising answer that the sand-blizzards at this time of year blotted out all communication on the surface of the planet; the sand was metallic and magnetic and wrecked all sorts of equipment. Nevertheless, I pinned all my hopes on Varzil's ability to fly the *dikri* saucer.

Karsten, too, was eager to get away. At the polar dome, which was a Federation Observatory, there were almost all the comforts of home. There would also be a chance, I gathered, to send a message to the mother ship about Rellin's illegal activities on Earth.

As for me, although I looked forward to the extra comforts of the Branntol Confederation base, I was still on Mars, and it wasn't my world. I had no idea when I could be sent back to Earth, if ever. Questioning Varzil was very unsatisfactory; I gathered that it was a question now of scheduling of the larger ships. A saucer *could* fly between Earth and Mars, but it seemed to be on a par with sailing a fifteen-foot sail-boat across the Atlantic: nothing anyone would do except for adventure or in a desperate emergency.

At last, Karsten's arm was healed enough, and Varzil felt familiar enough with the *dikri* saucer, to make the attempt. We got into our foul and dirty clothing again – there was water, but not enough for washing – and went down the narrow and steep steps into the vaulted cave where the *dikri* kept their saucer parked.

Varzil had been inside many times, but neither Karsten nor I had yet stepped inside the alien craft. As I walked up the ramp I felt the now-familiar twinge of fear.

It was completely unlike the saucer of Varzil and company. The door unlocked by the same dragon-shaped key; there was a long metal corridor, slightly curving, with a door on either side. One of these doors opened into a storeroom, with bunks and closed cabinets. The other led into a control chamber with panels and instruments.

Varzil said gravely, 'You will have to handle the navigation, Karsten; I shall have enough to do with the controls. My arms are not as strong as those of a *dikri* and the control levers will demand all my strength.'

Karsten looked serious and older. 'I think I can manage. But wouldn't it be safer for you to navigate and allow me to steer? You know your heart is not good.'

'And your arm is still weak,' Varzil told him. 'You haven't the strength.' They looked at me and I knew they were thinking of Harret. *If he had been with us* – their thought was almost audible – *instead of this weak native* . . . Well, it wasn't my fault I was here.

Varzil came to check if I was safely tied down. He said apologetically, 'The acceleration of take off in the *dikri* craft is much rougher than for human craft. I could not forgive myself if you were hurt.' He was so nice, all the time, and I must have been in the way.

'It's likely to be even rougher than usual,' Karsten said, his face grim, 'with us handling these controls.'

Varzil finished strapping himself in and bent to the controls. He touched something, and lights, glaringly bright, began to flicker on and off, then steadied to a greenish glare. He said, 'Hold on,' and reached for a lever. He began to move it slowly to one side.

A high, shrill roaring began in my ears. The craft leaped up and I felt myself flattened, squashed back against the cushions. I fought and gasped for breath, my eyes squeezed shut, struggled not to cry out with the pain of it, heard Karsten's involuntary scream. That shocked my eyes open; Karsten hadn't cried out at all during that ordeal in the desert . . .

Horror struck me. Varzil's face was drawn and darkly congested, and he had slumped limp against the retaining straps, his hands fallen from the lever. The lights oscillated wildly, bright to dim and bright again. Karsten tore at his straps, crying out incoherently, wrenched at the lever. The squashing pressure lessened, grew again, died away. The bottom dropped out of the world, and my stomach lurched and swam; we were falling, falling like stones; we would crash . . . I shut my eyes and waited for the smash. Karsten screamed again as we struck, and I saw him flung down hard, and then we jolted, bounced, and dropped again with a crash that brought my head forward against the bars violently.

I shook my head dazedly, got out of my straps – the cabin was tilted at a crazy angle – and struggled across the swaying floor to Karsten. For a ghastly moment I was afraid they were both dead; then Karsten sat up. His face was covered with blood, but otherwise he seemed none the worse.

'What happened?' I asked in a daze.

'We crashed,' Karsten said tersely. 'My father's heart – I do not know if he is alive.'

Even now I don't like thinking about those ten minutes before Varzil's faint pulse began to rally and his eyelids flickered. We got him out of his straps and I went down the metal corridor and opened the door so I could see how far we had fallen from the shelter. To my infinite relief it was less than five hundred yards.

Carrying him between us, sheltering him as best we could against the rising wind, Karsten and I were too anxious for despair. We got him inside, rubbed his wrists, poured hot drinks down his throat, and when he finally opened his eyes and knew us, I was almost as relieved as Karsten.

'The saucer isn't damaged,' Karsten told him quickly. 'We can try again.'

Varzil said, moving his lips with difficulty, 'I should not – have tried. I should – have taught Barry to handle the controls; he is strong. Before next try I will do so.' He slept again, exhausted by these few words; but he'd given me plenty to think about during the long hours before he spoke again.

But before Varzil could sit up again, we had something else to think about.

The wind here in the mountains, roaring round the shelter, was noisier than that deadly, silent wind on the desert plain. It was so perpetual that you stopped hearing it. Now, suddenly, I began hearing it again. The normal roaring sound was now an almost deafening howl, roaring round the corners of the little shelter, which was round and streamlined to offer as little resistance as possible. Varzil lay listening to it; he looked grave. Finally be broke the bad news.

'That is a full-scale sand-blizzard,' he said, and his tired face looked a hundred years old. 'We cannot try again, if the winter season has set in. Nothing can survive that, no craft. We must stay here until the winter season is over.'

Apprehension struck me cold, and I hardly heard my own voice as I asked, 'How long does the Martian winter last?'

'Fourteen of your months.'

CHAPTER ELEVEN

There's no sense in going into the events of that winter too deeply. There was nothing we could do except stay there. We stayed, and that was that.

The omnipresent worry about a *dikri* coming home unexpectedly and saying, 'Who's been sleeping in my bed,' like one of the Three Bears, eased off a little. We had to conserve water, and were always a little thirsty, but not dangerously so. The wind had occasional twenty-to-thirty-minute lulls, and then Karsten or I would make a dash outside for fresh supplies of lichen – there was plenty of it – to put to soak. We rigged a lifeline from the shelter so that neither of us would get lost if we estimated the time wrong and the sand began to howl again. If we'd been caught out more than a hundred feet from the shelter, in that roaring inferno of sand, we'd never have made it back. As it was, I lost the sight of one eye for almost ten days after getting caught outside. The sand was like emery powder; I knew enough to cover my face with both hands, but I had to put one hand down to open the door, and that did it. Fortunately Karsten had enough fresh clean water so that I could bathe it within seconds after getting in, and though I spent a nervous scared ten days, finally the soreness healed and I could see again. Varzil told us it was fortunate there were three of us; it had long been known that no two beings could endure being crammed together in confined space for months without going mad. I didn't argue. I thought three was bad enough. We got fairly sick of each other's company, I suppose, and yet – after a few months I began to realize that if I had to be cooped up with *somebody*, it could have been worse.

We talked a lot, just to have something to do. At Varzil's suggestion, I whiled away the time, when it was my turn to talk, by trying to remember every scrap I knew of Earth's history and telling them all I knew. They were a little surprised that I knew only the history of one continent thoroughly, and the rest sketchily, and I felt a little ashamed at the superficial quality of my knowledge. In my lighter moments I tried to reconstruct such things as *Alice in Wonderland* so I could join in the story telling; and we searched our minds for all the old jokes we knew.

Varzil had only waited for enough strength to be able to talk again before starting to teach both Karsten and me, from rough-sketched diagrams, how to control the *dikri* ship. I think he was preparing us in case he had another attack and died here in the shelter. When he found out how poor I was in maths, he insisted on starting in, right then, to teach me.

I thought it was all I could do to count my change; that if I couldn't manage the maths of Earth I certainly couldn't manage that of the Galactic Confederation.

I learned anyhow.

Varzil decided that I'd had bad grounding in arithmetic as a kid and went back to the kindergarten stages and taught me all over again. It was easier after that. He gave me a lot of mental shortcuts and tricks which made it seem easy. And besides, there wasn't another damn thing to do.

They took me up through arithmetic, algebra and trigonometry, with the help of the pocket tables they carried on them. Varzil also had a slide rule, and when I expressed surprise, he told me that it was a simpler form of one known in the Galactic civilization; the principle was the same, but the Earth one was just handier to carry in a pocket. It took only a few minutes to learn to convert from one form of figures to the other. Having ten fingers, they also used maths to a base of ten, but they taught me to use a twelve-based one 'for convenience', and a three-based one 'as a mental recreation'; then they began to teach me celestial and sidereal navigation. By the time eight months were up we had run out of ordinary maths, and they started to go into complicated subjects like hyperspace orbit computation and mass-time star-drift. Varzil was an astronomer, and I ought to add that Karsten didn't know all these subjects either, when I caught up with him, he did lessons right along with me.

If I ever got back to Earth, I guessed, I wouldn't *miss* the year of school I was missing. I'd have the equivalent of a Ph.D. in maths!

The maths was fascinating, but just the same, we hung over that calender. We were all a mess. I'd lost about twelve or fourteen pounds – the lichen was pretty good, even as a steady diet, but you got tired of it and it didn't tempt you to fatten up. As for washing, we didn't, except just enough to keep our skin barely endurable. It's surprising how little you *can* wash, and how much you miss that daily bath when you can't have it. As far as our clothes were concerned they were crusted with dirt, and Karsten and I were growing out of our jeans and going through the elbows of our shirts.

Early in the winter we had found cabinets with utility coveralls hanging inside; they had the loathsome *dikri* dragon-shape insignia on them and we shuddered away from them, but after five months of wearing the same clothes every day and sleeping in them at night, you'll wear almost anything. Karsten and I finally decided we would wear the *dikri* coveralls, provided there wasn't a *dikri* in them. The alternative would have been a loincloth, and it was too cold for that.

The *dikri* garments had one advantage; they were almost completely windproof. We could go out in them for lichen, or sand for the oxygen converters, without getting frozen to the bone.

The great day came when Varzil said it would be safe to try again for the Polar colony, and we looked again at our filthy, sand-grimed Earth clothes, and put on the *dikri* garments, then Karsten grabbed the *dikri* insignia sewn on his coverall front, and pulled. It tore, then came loose.

'There!' he said violently, and I followed suit. It felt better, not having the damned dragon *on* us.

We didn't say much. We had discussed everything about the flight. We found the saucer where we had crash-landed it. Long before, we had made sure there was no gross damage, and if there was hidden damage – well, there was nothing we could do about repairing it, so we'd have to trust to luck. This time Varzil was strapped, tenderly, into the spare seat, and Karsten and I took our seat before the flight levers. I felt solemn and scared, but mostly just eager to get going. Karsten was going to navigate; I was going to handle the controls. I'd practised, 'dry', on a sketched mock-up inside the shelter, and I thought I knew how to do it. It wasn't much different from driving a car, I thought, as I thrust the small brass dragon-key into the main power switch lock. There was an instant flare of green light, a shudder of power, a surge of acceleration. I hauled at the lever – it took all my strength – and we were airborne over Mars.

I relaxed, I could do it. I was flying the thing. I drew as much breath as I could against the acceleration, and Karsten, his face pale with pride, grinned at me.

'Here goes for the Polar colony,' he murmured, 'and if I see the Martian hills again, on the Last Day of All, it will be too soon for me!'

'Them's my sentiments exactly,' I quoted, and concentrated on a lever again. The instruments read the correct course. Speeds were calculated by a complex system with no Earth references, but I knew we would arrive at the Polar colony within six or seven hours.

For the first time in a long time, I felt good. This was the first step on my long road home. I fully expected to be at the Polar colony, and find that Karsten and I were the heroes of the hour.

It was astonishing how easy it was to fly the little craft. We hit some wind-buffeting as we crossed the equator, and went up above the limits of the atmosphere, finding that above the level of the sand-clouds the sun was colourless again, though still small and cold. We sighted the Polar colony through the viewing panel while we were still miles away, and began slowly to lower our saucer towards it.

We were hovering above the dome at about eight hundred feet when Karsten, who had been quieter and quieter, finally pointed downwards towards the tip of the dome.

'Look,' he said in a low voice. 'Father, unstrap your belts and come here. You must see this.'

Varzil approached as we hovered, lowering, over the field, and I realized that I was caught in the nightmare again.

Only once had I seen a big *dikri* ship; as we stood abandoned on the Martian desert, expecting death momentarily, watching as they left us there. The shape was printed indelibly on my heart.

And down below, over the Confederation dome, there were at least a dozen of them.

The Polar colony was in the hands of the *dikri*.

CHAPTER TWELVE

We didn't have to discuss it. We swung ship and got out of there fast, hoping it was fast enough. I didn't know what had happened. Neither did Varzil.

'It could be war,' he said, 'or they could have decided to – eliminate the base. If there were no Confederation personnel in this Sector, and if the Confederation ship had gone home, they might be ignored by the Confederation for a considerable period of time. The Confederation might simply believe that the Polar colony had been wiped out by volcanic eruptions or some natural disaster, and not trouble to send replacements. It is not easy to get volunteers for re-staffing a colony on such an inhospitable world.'

Karsten's mouth worked. 'Are we going to let them do this?'

'My dear son, how can we prevent them?' Varzil sat back, looking very old. 'We cannot communicate with any ship in this system – or anywhere else – without our own equipment. Half of that was in the saucer the *dikri* stole from us; the other half, on Earth. You and I have probably long been listed as dead, along with Harret.'

Karsten flared, 'We could take this saucer back to Earth!'

Varzil's eyes sparked briefly, then he said, 'Too dangerous.'

I finally spoke up. 'You told me it's been done,

even with Confederation small craft – and this is larger and more stable.'

'And I know it less well,' Varzil said. 'No, it is impossible. The only safe thing is to return to the shelter–'

'And wait for the *dikri* to remember the place, and come and polish us off? It seems to me we're dead either way,' Karsten said angrily. 'Let's give them a run for their money! Barry, are you willing to try?'

I wasn't. I was scared to death, remembering that Varzil had told me it was like sailing a small boat round the Horn. But neither did I want to go back to the shelter to starve, freeze and eventually die there. I said firmly, 'I've learned enough maths for one winter!'

'Are you willing to take the chance of playing tag with the *dikri* ships if they spot us en route?' Varzil demanded. Karsten and I looked at each other, and finally nodded, first at one another, then at Varzil.

The old man sighed.

'Then I have nothing to say,' he said. 'You have grown up, both of you. You must do the flying. There are emergency rations on board, *dikri* rations, but we will not die of that. I am an old man; it is you who will do the work, so you must make the decision. I am in your hands.'

Karsten and I kept looking at each other. It was an awfully big step to take. Finally Karsten said, 'Now they have taken the Polar colony, what will they do to this world if it is not reported?'

'And where will they strike next?' I nodded. I knew more about the *dikri* than I'd known fourteen months ago.

I want it clear; I wasn't playing Save the Universe.

I just wanted to get home – and I wanted to spike the *dikri*'s guns. I think Karsten felt much the same way. We just looked at each other and nodded. Then Karsten started to unfasten his belts.

'Change places with me,' he said. 'Father, you strap yourself in. Barry, I'll take the controls on the first watch – and you set a course for Earth. We'll have to allow for orbital change.'

That was all there was to it. With no more fuss than that, the *dikri* saucer became an interplanetary ship, and we were in command.

Laying a course for Earth was easy. What wasn't easy was the knowledge that we were doing this in an unfamiliar ship, not really fitted for such a trip; that even Varzil was very uncertain about some of the emergency equipment. There is a big difference between navigating, and manipulating, a craft like this over the Martian desert, and navigating it on the long orbit between Earth and Mars, flying the tricky and unpredictable solar magnetic currents. It was going to take both of us to run the ship for this trip, which would take a minimum of four days or a maximum of six. We were going to be short of sleep.

Karsten spoke my thoughts aloud. 'No automatic pilot, which means we have to manhandle the thing all the way.'

Manhandle was the right word. There was a three-dimensional compass in a transparent bubble, lined up on the Sun and Polaris, and you had to haul sets of heavy levers up and down to keep the ship in a spin oriented to your bearing in three dimensions. This was intended for a fast and manoeuvrable small craft, not limited by the speeds and directions of freefall orbits, but it was clumsy and hard to handle compared to a Confederation saucer; I realized that the *dikri* must have incredible physical strength.

There was another thing we didn't talk about. *Dikri* craft were coming and going all around Mars. If one of them spotted us – we'd had it.

I didn't know then, but I could have guessed, that the journey back to Earth was to haunt me in nightmares for months, years afterwards. Now and then, for a short time, Varzil came to take the auxiliary seat, so that Karsten or I could grab a fitful doze; but long before we sighted the small grey-greenish ball that was Earth in the viewer, we were both staggering with fatigue. In desperation, I rigged up a sort of alarm device; if my head fell backwards, a buzzer shocked me awake again. Twice, we saw flickers on the scanning screens which we were sure were *dikri* ships, but either we were mistaken, or they didn't see us.

I was at the controls when the levers began to fight my arms, and Karsten, white-faced, helped me to haul on them. Through gasps he panted, 'We're beginning to get inside the gravity field – I'll cut the power down as far as I can–'

'How does this thing handle inside atmosphere? I don't want to set down in Tibet or the middle of the Pacific Ocean,' I gasped. Without wasting breath he got a hand loose and pointed to the planetary field-scanner below, with latitude and longitude lines. It wasn't a fine adjustment. I supposed the *dikri*, familiar with these craft, flew by something analogous to visual flight rules, knowing where they wanted to go. I wasn't even too sure of the latitude and longitude of San Francisco.

The planet grew and grew in our viewscreen, swelling and swelling, seeming to rush towards us, hurtling through dead-black sky, which gradually paled and lightened. It felt a little like a ride on a too-fast roller coaster. We were skimming the magnetic currents around the planet now, making a fast pass into atmosphere, dipping out again before the decrease in speed could burn up the hull, gradually braking down with the atmosphere as our skid-brake. It was rough and bumpy and we were all sore and bruised despite restraining belts. It was lousy ship-handling and lousy navigation; we were aiming roughly at the lower Pacific edge of the North American continent. If we were lucky that would put us somewhere in California. If it weren't, we might have to hike back from South of the Border – or we might even take a nice long bath, and not the kind we'd been dreaming about all those endless months on Mars.

I felt the same strange, deathly clarity I had felt when we were almost dying of cold and thirst in the desert. Things were happening too fast after those long, long, dragging months. I didn't expect to be alive an hour from that minute. We managed somehow to skid down and hover, wobbling, five thousand feet above land. At least we weren't over the Pacific. Now all we had to do was pick a nice deserted area to land in. And then Karsten gasped and poked me in the ribs, without the breath to speak.

'*Dikri* craft!'

They hovered before us, small, deadly and grey, spinning in that momentary pause before rushing in. Karsten and I hit the levers almost together and got away from there, fast; but almost before we felt the surge of acceleration we knew we were lost. They were fresh, they knew how to handle their ships, they had everything going for them. I began to think I'd rather crash.

The ship swayed and seemed to roll silently beneath us. The straps cut into my belly with the force of acceleration. Behind, us, far astern and yet gaining, came the three *dikri* saucers.

Then, almost at the last minute, something roared off our bows and swung around with a thunder of jets. Two enormous military jets, swept-winged, huge, so strangely and dearly familiar that I wanted to cry, roared past – and I saw the *dikri* ships stop, with that unbelievable hovering motion in fast midflight – which is so unthinkable to anyone flying conventional planes, jet or rockets – reverse, and whisk out of sight. I hardly believed it. Karsten said, between his dry lips, 'Saved by a couple of Strategic Air Command planes. Those pilots will have fun chasing them and then go back to base and be called damned liars by their commanders. I'd like to send them all a bottle of whisky or a bunch of roses or something!'

Chasing the three saucers, the planes disappeared and we cautiously lowered our craft further and further. There was a wide open desert-like patch of country, with clumps of low green Joshua trees, visible now as wavery green. We hauled back at the levers, and with the last of our strength managed to set the craft down.

We were back on Earth. Fifteen months after we had left it, after the most incredible adventure anyone had known, I was home again. I felt dead and empty. 'What now?'

'Now,' said Varzil, 'we hide the saucer – the *dikri*

must not find it again – and try to get to the nearest town.' He gestured to Karsten to unfasten his straps. Karsten asked anxiously, 'can you walk, Father?'

'I can do anything I have to do.' Varzil pulled himself upright. He looked dead beat, but he smiled, a very likeable smile. 'I told you, Barry, that we would bring you back at the earliest opportunity. I am sorry that it took just a little longer than I foresaw.'

That did it. We all stood there and howled with laughter until we were weak.

But I still felt anxious. We were wearing the *dikri* uniforms, and they would pass as normal coveralls or Army fatigues, and I supposed Varzil had some money. But I didn't even know what state we were in, and there still remained the problem of the *dikri*, flying around in their saucers.

I asked, a little anxiously, 'What will you do now?'

Varzil said, 'We must hide the *dikri* saucer. We will need it later. You see, I had, even in the Berkeley house, no transmitter; it is forbidden to install such a powerful transmitter on a planet without official Galactic representation. We're here more or less unofficially, you know, for scientific study; but it means I am strictly forbidden to do anything to reveal myself to the authorities of your planet. However, there are three other scientists here on a similar project, though none of them have a small craft like my saucer which the *dikri* captured. If I can reach one of them, I can pick up a signal from the receivers they will have. Receivers are allowed, you see. It will tell me if there is a Confederation ship in the system, or when one will arrive, and I can take the *dikri* saucer up, rendezvous with it, and make my delayed report – and go home.'

That had only one disadvantage. 'Will your Confederation ship be willing to rendezvous in space with a *dikri* craft? Won't they shoot you down, thinking you're a *dikri*?'

Karsten said, patiently, 'They won't shoot anybody down. They'll probably think we are *dikri* wanting a conference, or to surrender. They will be surprised, but they won't hurt us, and when we board, they'll find out their mistake.'

Meanwhile, we had to find the other scientists from Varzil's home world; and I was getting pretty anxious. I said, 'The first thing *I've* got to do is to telephone my parents. I've been missing for more than a year, and they must think I'm dead – or that I've joined the Foreign Legion or something.' I felt sick and a little trembly. What was I going to tell them?

The saucer was, of course, mounted on rollers, which made it easy to slide into the bushes. A passing truck driver gave the three of us a lift without asking any questions. A few very careful questions from me told us that we were in Texas. *Well,* I thought glumly, *we only missed California by about nine hundred miles.*

The truck dropped us near the edge of a small Texas city whose name I wasn't sure of. Before I could call my family, I realized, I'd have to find out where I was! We stood for a moment not speaking, getting adjusted to being safe back on Earth.

It was frightfully hot. We had become so accustomed to the bitter cold of Mars, and the even more bitter cold of the unheated spacecraft, that we all felt weak and the sweat poured down our faces. I was coming slowly to terms with the awareness that I was safe, I was back home, in a few minutes I might hear my parents' voices. I felt strangely torn; this was the end of something, for it was unlikely that I would ever see Karsten or Varzil again.

Karsten broke the strange, tense silence between us. He said, 'Pardon me for being so prosaic at this fateful moment, but I'm hungry. Father, you had some American money when we left; did the *dikri* take it from you?'

'They took nothing,' Varzil said. 'It was so long ago I had almost forgotten. I suggest we all find ourselves a meal.'

Ordering a large and varied meal in the little café, we attracted no attention, or so I thought. I went to the telephone, and tried to call my parents in Berkeley, but I heard the phone ringing in the empty house, and felt almost sick with frustration. I kept saying to myself, *I've waited fourteen months, I can wait a few hours longer*, but it didn't help.

Karsten kept looking anxiously around, and finally Varzil sharply told him to sit still. 'You are acting like a child!'

Karsten said, almost inaudibly, 'There is someone looking through the window at us. I think it is a Changer.'

'You have *dikri* on the brain,' I told him with exasperation. 'If they think of us at all, they think we're long dead on Mars.'

'Yes, even if they saw us land,' Varzil said, 'they would think we were one of their own.' He looked tired, tired to exhaustion. I hated to think of him trying to fly the *dikri* saucer up to their mother ship. I hated to think of the imminent parting, and yet I, too, was eager to get home. I realized I was going to miss them, and I felt angry with myself for getting so emotional about the whole thing. I ate fried chicken with dogged insistence, staring at my plate. In a few minutes I'd try to call Berkeley again.

Kartsten said sharply, in a whisper, 'There is that – man – again!'

I twisted around. The man was short and thick-set and he did seem to be staring at us. A *dikri* in the human metamorphosis? Or just an ordinary, ugly man? We probably looked like three beat-up tramps in the worn *dikri* uniforms. But Karsten said urgently, 'Father! Are you weaponed? Our rods would function again, in the field of the planet–'

'Keep your voice down!' Varzil ordered. 'What is the matter with you, Karsten? Yes, I took one of the *dikri* weapons from the saucer. But I'm not going to use it here!' He paid the bill for the meal and we left the little café.

It was getting dark, the sun huge and red at the flat horizon between the low buildings. Varzil said, 'We may have to spend the night here, if Barry cannot reach his parents at once. As for us, we must locate–'

He broke off, for a thick, unmistakable voice behind us said, 'Don't move!'

Nevertheless, I moved. I might have known.

Karsten said, 'Rellin!' in a voice of hatred and loathing.

The *dikri* looked smug, if human feelings could be transmitted to such a face. It said, 'Looking for a small craft here without permission, I discover an old enemy. No, Varzil–' It swung the weapon in its hand towards the older man. 'I am curious how you got here. You seem to be my evil genius. However, since you have long been considered dead–'

'My corpse,' Varzil said softly. 'How will you move it through the streets here, or account for my being found dead months after my supposed death?'

Rellin paused for only a moment, but in that moment I leaped. I thought, *If I can hurt it, if I can make it do that dragon-changing stunt right here on the street, it won't dare stay around where anyone can find it.* At the same moment, as Rellin stepped back before my leap, Varzil drew his weapon and fired. There was a bright blue flash and pain seared along my leg.

Karsten shouted 'Help! Help!' and I heard the sound of running feet, shouts and cries. Rellin had staggered back against a lamp post and its flesh writhed, moved, but with what must have been fearful effort it maintained the human shape. It snarled deep in its throat, and I braced myself for the terrible dragon-rush, but instead it swung towards Karsten and raised its weapon.

I shouted 'No, Rellin!' and charged.

Something struck my head like a thousand tons of TNT and I fell a million miles into outer space and disappeared.

Part III

CHAPTER THIRTEEN

My head felt as if it were bursting.

I opened my eyes to see Karsten bending over me, his eyes anxious and worried. I said, 'This seems to be where I came in.'

He said, in a low frightened voice, 'Barry, Rellin went – and took the girl with it! Are you all right? Have you still got the key?'

My head spinning, I sat up. Time kaleidoscoped, slid together, and I remembered where I was: in the Abilene motel, with Lisa Barnard–

Lisa! Lisa was gone – and Rellin had her!

Karsten said, white-faced, 'I couldn't stop them; Rellin said it would kill the girl unless I let it go.'

I hauled myself to my feet. 'Where did they go?'

'I think Rellin's heading for the saucer. You know – where we hid it, outside of town. That was why I had to stay here; to make sure no one from your planet had found it. Rellin has my father, Barry; I think it's hidden him aboard!'

Confused, I pulled myself together. 'Lisa's car is outside! Come on – if you know the way to the saucer, I can follow them!'

We ran for the car; fortunately Lisa had left the key in the ignition, and seconds later we were speeding along the highway out of town. At Karsten's direction I swung on to a country road and headed southwards.

Karsten said, 'You know me now!'

'Yes – but how did I get into the hospital?'

Karsten quickly filled me in. 'When you fell, Rellin swung its weapon on us – but evidently someone had heard the sounds of the fight and called the police. We heard sirens, and Rellin ran. My father and I ran, too; we were afraid of being questioned. I knew they would find you and take care of you. I was afraid Rellin would find us and take the key from us, so my father stuck it in the pocket of your coverall– Here, turn, this way.'

My foot pressed the accelerator and Lisa's car roared. I felt sick and shaken at the thought of Lisa in the hands of the *dikri.* True, Varzil had told me they would not normally dare to interfere with a native of a planet under observation, like Earth. But Rellin had broken law after law; it might be desperate enough to feel that a dead witness was safer than a live one.

I said, 'Have you been here all this time?'

'Yes – my father collapsed, after the fight with Rellin, and was seriously ill; I had to find a place to stay, and care for him. We were able to find a compatriot, here to study meteors, and he sent us a little money for expenses. Twice I tried to call your house in Berkeley and leave a message, but I was not able to reach you. I did find out, from the hospital, that someone had come to take you home. Father was very ill – we could not even think of leaving and in any case you had the key to the saucer.'

'He is better now, though?'

'Oh, yes,' Karsten said, 'but – not very strong. He needs care, and rest, and peace of mind. He has been through too much.'

So have you, I thought, looking at Karsten's drawn

face in the darkness, but I didn't say so. I only said, 'How will you get home?'

'My father's scientist friend tells me that there is a Confederation ship just beyond the orbit of the moon; it moved away during the last months to keep clear of your moonshot satellites, but now it has come back. If we had the saucer, and the key–'

'We'll do our damnedest about the saucer,' I said between my teeth. 'Where is that hiding place?'

'Turn at this cotton patch,' Karsten instructed, 'and you'd better turn off the headlights.'

I switched off, slackening speed as I did so. We neared a clump of trees and bushes, and stopped. Karsten got out, closing the door very quietly, and pointed.

'The saucer is hidden there,' he whispered, 'and Rellin must have taken the girl aboard.'

We thrust through the brushwood, flinching at the mesquite thorns that tore our faces, tensed against the sound of our own footsteps.

The saucer rose against the darkness, a darker loom in the night. If Varzil and the girl were in there, they might almost as well be on Mars for all we could do for them. And yet I had to try. Lisa had been the first friendly voice in that dreadful time when I had lost myself. Varzil – Varzil had kept us alive during that trek across the Martian desert, which even now seemed like a nightmare. Now that I saw the *dikri* saucer again, now that I remembered that awful ordeal of cold and hunger and pain, the nightmarish flight and the horror of the *dikri*, I wanted to turn tail and run, to say to Karsten: *This isn't my fight, I got into it by accident; this time I'm staying out of it.* And yet if I did I knew I'd lose something worse than my memory. Karsten kept silent, and so did I, calculating our chances.

It was just crazy enough to work. Rellin wouldn't be expecting us, if we were lucky. It would think, with its hostages, it could take off in peace and quiet, and dispose of them as it saw fit. My own impulse, to call out the cops – or the Air Force – died almost as soon as I thought of it. Sure, if they saw the flying saucer right in front of their eyes, they'd believe me. They'd probably even help rescue Lisa.

But then what? Political complications, maybe even interplanetary war! We here on Earth simply weren't ready for a Galactic civilization.

We took a few cautious steps up the ramp. Nobody shot at us.

I whispered, 'Are you sure Rellin is here?'

'It has come here before.'

We went on up the ramp. I was shaking. Suppose Rellin, who certainly must have a spacecraft key of its own, decided to shake us off once and for all by taking off while we were halfway up the ramp? We reached the door, and pushed against it.

It was locked.

That didn't matter. I had a key which would fit it. But if we walked in–

Suddenly the blaze of an idea flared in my mind. I remembered the controls of the *dikri* ship, as Varzil had taught me. Quickly, I jammed the key into the outside lock. 'The safety device,' I told Karsten. 'Remember? All hatches have to be closed and locked shut. With the key still in the door, this hatch is locked open – and Rellin can't take off!'

We left the lock jammed, and stole down the narrow metal corridor. With a strange sense of *déjà vu,* I recognized my dream. No wonder I thought I had spent some time on a submarine!

We paused at the cabin door. I heard a cry from inside, and started to rush it, but Karsten held me back.

'Let me go! Lisa–'

'We can't rush Rellin, or it'll kill my father and the girl,' Karsten said. 'I have a weapon–' He showed me the narrow glass rod I had seen that night in Berkeley. 'We have to get them out of firing range somehow.'

We stood in the corridor, indecisive. All sorts of crazy plans spun in my head and were rejected; to set the saucer on fire, to yell and hide till he came out to find us–

'I have it,' I whispered, shoving Karsten towards the second door. I remembered that this led into a room filled with stored equipment and bunks. 'When Rellin finds out the lock is jammed, and can't take off, it'll come to investigate–'

We stood flattened inside the metal door as the lights began to flicker on and off. Rellin was preparing a take-off, and I was sure Karsten was right about what Rellin planned: to leave the atmosphere of Earth and dispose of the hostages in space. I tensed against the eerie fear, the flickering lights. If we were wrong, if Rellin did not bother to investigate the jammed lock, if it took off anyhow, we would be flung around, without safety belts, like eggs in a freight car.

The lights flickered again; there was a soft whining metallic sound, then the creak of a door, and the hideous dragon-head, incongruous above an ordinary business suit too small for the grotesque form, thrust through the door. Karsten yelled, fired twice in rapid succession; there was an inhuman horrid howl, the howl of a *dikri* in anguish, and it whirled with that terrible unstoppable energy and charged us. Karsten fired again; I threw myself down into a crouch and butted, hard, with my head. Rellin went down, howling, twitched and lay still, convulsing.

I asked, 'Is it dead?'

'No,' Karsten said between his teeth, 'but give me time.'

But I left him standing over Rellin and burst into the cabin. Varzil, slumped against safety straps, said my name weakly as I came in, but I had eyes only for Lisa, white and terrified in the seat. I unstrapped her and helped her up.

'Take it easy,' I said with rough tenderness. 'The Marines have landed, and the situation is well in hand, or something like that. Don't yell; just give me one of your nylons or something. We've got somebody to tie up.'

You've got to hand it to that girl. She didn't even ask the million questions that must have been on the tip of her tongue. She just bent down and stripped off one of her nurse's white nylons, and I tossed it to Karsten.

'Here,' I said, 'the bursting strength of these things is probably more than even a *dikri* can manage. Tie the damned thing up.' Varzil was weakly unfastening his own straps, and I said, 'Go and help him, or Karsten's likely to strangle it, and I don't imagine you want that.'

'No,' said Varzil grimly, 'Rellin will return to the Confederation headquarters with us, to stand trial for murder and attempted murder – and the

Confederation will deal with the *dikri* at the Polar colony.'

I held Lisa back so that she would not see the dragon. But when I thrust my head into the corridor Rellin was human again, with bleeding face and torn clothing: only a tall, slab-faced man, the man I had known, briefly, as Roland.

I had not remembered him. But my unconscious mind had known. It had been wiped clean of everything save fear.

'Why,' Lisa said in wonder, coming into the corridor behind me, 'it's Mr Roland. Then he *wasn't* your father, Barry!' She stared at me. 'What sort of crazy game of international spies–'

'I don't know,' I said. 'I was always the innocent bystander.'

I couldn't even try to tell her, now. She deserved some explanation; but the true one was too fantastic for the moment. I said, 'Lisa, will you get out and wait in your car? I'll be with you in a minute.'

I stood in the hallway while they fastened Rellin into a seat, locking it firmly so that when it recovered strength, it could not escape. Varzil retrieved the key from the outside lock and said, 'And now we must go. There is no great hurry – the mother ship from the Confederation will remain in this system throughout the next fortnight – but I confess I am eager to be on home territory. And now that I know you are safe, Barry, there is nothing to keep us.'

I faced them both, hating to say goodbye. We had been through so much together; they seemed somehow closer than family to me. I had found them again and now, irrevocably, there was this parting. My throat lumped up, and I could hardly speak.

Karsten, too, seemed moved. He swallowed hard and said, 'Why don't you come with us? We could get a permit for you–'

For a moment the temptation grew wildly in me. I had only gone the first step into space. There was so much I did not know. To see the stars– Then I shook my head firmly. I couldn't do that to my family. Not again.

Varzil said, 'Barry. Keep your eyes open. I will give your name to our other contacts in this star system; there are a few natives of this planet who know of our existence; it is helpful to us to have friends here. And' – a smile broke over his drawn face – 'in a few years, we will be back. I have not yet completed my work here.'

'And if he doesn't come back,' Karsten said firmly, 'I will – and I'll see you then!' He held out his hand, then suddenly, roughly, hugged me. 'I'm going to miss you,' he said. 'I'm going to miss you like the devil!'

I was going to miss him too. A big hunk of my life was going with them. My eyes were stinging as I stumbled down the ramp, alone, and heard the door of the saucer lock behind me, cold, irrevocable, shutting me out forever from the world of my adventure.

By the time I reached Lisa's car, I had myself in hand again. She slid over from the wheel as I approached, saying. 'You drive. I can't without my shoes on.'

I took the wheel in silence, staring upwards at the pattern of lights which flickered blue, amber, green, rose silently higher and higher and disappeared. Then I put the car in gear and flicked on the headlights, and we got away from there. Lisa was silent all the way back to town. Finally she said, 'That crazy aeroplane of theirs – it looked almost like a flying saucer!'

And I knew what I must say.

'Don't be silly! You didn't see any little green men inside it, did you?'

'Do you want to go back to the motel where you were staying?' she asked. It sounded like a dead anti-climax. I turned to her and laughed. 'No. I've got no reason to go back there now. I might just as well catch a plane to Berkeley.' Then I stopped the car, pulling to the edge of the road, and laughed softly at her crestfallen face.

'I'll be back,' I promised. 'I've got something to come back for now.'

It had been a long, long time since I'd kissed a girl. It was about time I started getting back to myself. Now that I knew who I was – well, it had been a long time between girls.

EPILOGUE

It was raining in San Francisco when the plane landed, and they were all there to meet me: Father, grinning all over his face; Nina looking awfully glad to see me; and Win, small and very serious. I knew, when I saw them all, just how glad I was to be back, and just how afraid they must have been that I'd disappear again and never be heard of. It made me admire my father all over again. He'd known I might not come back – and yet he let me go. With a family like that, I might even be able to tell them the truth someday. But not now. They'd been through enough – and this burden would be too much. For now, it would be enough that I was back – and myself again.

My father held the car door open; Nina got into the back so that Win and I could sit up front. This had been the special treat when we were little kids, and I felt touched by it. I leaned over and kissed her on the cheek. She reached up her hand and patted me, then let me go and I got in, letting Win sit by the window.

Father started the car, then asked, 'Did you find out what you wanted to know, Barry?'

I nodded, and grinned at him. 'I found out.'

I knew I didn't have to tell him any more. Someday, when I could, I would, and he knew it; for now, if I didn't want to say anything, I knew he wouldn't ask. It felt wonderful. I was home.

It was Win who asked, 'Where *were* you all that time, Barry? Did you find out?'

I winked at her, put my arm around her and squeezed. 'As a matter of fact,' I said, dead pan, 'I got kidnapped on a flying saucer and they took me to Mars – and I had to wait till we could steal a saucer and fly back.'

'Oh, *you*!' She flounced away and stared out of the window, then, giggling a little, snuggled back against me and put her head on my shoulder. 'What did I do to have a brother like you?'

It was Nina, leaning over from the back seat, who asked the important question. She took my free hand, the one that wasn't around Win, and asked, 'But – you're really all right now, Barry?'

'Yes,' I said, knowing it was true. I had caught up with the lost year; I had lost myself and found myself again, and now it was time to go on to the next thing. Karsten would be back someday – and there were lots of flying saucers around.

'Yes,' I said again, 'I'm all right.'